The Executioner slowed and looked back at the American Embassy

Kinshasa might be boiling with political intrigue, but something Bolan had seen or heard in the CIA observation room had put him on edge.

The instant he stepped outside the gate, Bolan knew what it was. No fewer than three different factions watched the front of the embassy. By entering and leaving so openly he had become a target.

Quinn had let him become a new pawn in a game of political intrigue that he neither wanted nor had the time to deal with.

Bolan was diving for cover when the first bullet tried to find a home in his flesh. He rolled behind a burned-out car and came to his knees, reaching for his pistol. He scanned the area where the shots must have come from, but saw nothing. A quick glance in the direction of the embassy showed the marines were alert but not willing to come out to his aid.

The Executione

MACK BOLAN®
The Executioner

The Don Pendleton's Executioner®

FIRE ZONE

TORONTO • NEW YORK • LONDON
AMSTERDAM • PARIS • SYDNEY • HAMBURG
STOCKHOLM • ATHENS • TOKYO • MILAN
MADRID • WARSAW • BUDAPEST • AUCKLAND

Recycling programs
for this product may
not exist in your area.

First edition October 2009

ISBN-13: 978-0-373-64371-4

Special thanks and acknowledgment to
Russell Davis for his contribution to this work.

FIRE ZONE

Printed in U.S.A.

Fire is the test of gold; adversity of strong men.

—Seneca
c. 3 BC–AD 65

All that glitters isn't gold. Nobody can put a price on justice.

—Mack Bolan

THE MACK BOLAN LEGEND

Nothing less than a war could have fashioned the destiny of the man called Mack Bolan. Bolan earned the Executioner title in the jungle hell of Vietnam.

But this soldier also wore another name—Sergeant Mercy. He was so tagged because of the compassion he showed to wounded comrades-in-arms and Vietnamese civilians.

Mack Bolan's second tour of duty ended prematurely when he was given emergency leave to return home and bury his family, victims of the Mob. Then he declared a one-man war against the Mafia.

He confronted the Families head-on from coast to coast, and soon a hope of victory began to appear. But Bolan had broken society's every rule. That same society started gunning for this elusive warrior—to no avail.

So Bolan was offered amnesty to work within the system against terrorism. This time, as an employee of Uncle Sam, Bolan became Colonel John Phoenix. With a command center at Stony Man Farm in Virginia, he and his new allies—Able Team and Phoenix Force—waged relentless war on a new adversary: the KGB.

But when his one true love, April Rose, died at the hands of the Soviet terror machine, Bolan severed all ties with Establishment authority.

Now, after a lengthy lone-wolf struggle and much soul-searching, the Executioner has agreed to enter an "arm's-length" alliance with his government once more, reserving the right to pursue personal missions in his Everlasting War.

Prologue

It was a perfect day to start a forest fire.

The weather in Idaho had been dry all summer long, the result of an overly aggressive La Niña drying up the usual rains that made the mountains come alive with greenery. What was, in good years, a hillside covered with ponderosa pine and juniper now stretched as dry as a tinderbox, not quite brown but far from the vibrant green that the Boise National Forest usually enjoyed. The camo-dressed man moved swiftly through the woods with his twenty-pound pack, heavy footsteps crunching dried pine needles.

He held up a GPS unit to better see the display and adjusted his path according to the satellite-sent information until he came to an area that looked like any other at the edge of a meadow. But this was the spot. The Spot.

He shrugged off the backpack and let it fall to the ground, placing the GPS beside it to verify the exact location. Even with the enhanced number of satellites—he needed at least three for a proper fix—he couldn't get closer than three yards to the spot. For what he intended, this was good enough. Dropping to his knees, he rummaged through the pack and pulled out two plastic-wrapped boxes the size of bread loaves. He carefully placed each on the forest floor in a pattern he had practiced until it was second nature. Drawing out the last box required more finesse, since it contained the PETN detonators.

As he stripped off the plastic wrapping from the det cord

laid into the packages like snowy white intestines, he froze. The wind had died, but his keen hearing picked up sounds from a hundred yards away.

Laughter. Snippets of a bawdy song wailed by a man with a baritone voice, followed by a higher-pitched woman's complaint. The complaint disappeared suddenly, replaced by a baritone laugh and girlish giggles. He was not alone.

Tipping his head to one side, he homed in on the two hikers moving across a meadow in front of him. Fading back into the forest and letting them pass was out of the question. A quick check of his watch showed that the deadline was rushing down on him. He touched his earbud and considered calling Red Leader. The thought passed as quickly as it had come to him. He knew what Red Leader would say—and it would scorch his ass.

Leaving his partially unwound det cord and blasting caps where he had placed them on the ground, he stood and reached behind to the small of his back. His fingers closed on a sheathed KA-BAR knife. He watched the hikers steadily approaching. As he had thought, a boy and a girl, maybe not out of their teens, intent on an afternoon communing with nature and each other.

The girl saw him first and tugged at her boyfriend's arm. The boy half turned, misinterpreted her intentions and tried to kiss her. She ducked away and avoided his lips, speaking rapidly.

The boy turned and looked across the meadow. His shoulders slumped in resignation at the realization that what he sought most in the national forest was not going to be found as soon as he had hoped.

"Hello!" the boy called in an attempt to make the most of his bad luck.

The man in camo stood silently, hand behind his back, fingers lightly circling the hilt of the knife. For all his outward composure, inside he seethed. He was going to be behind schedule. Red Leader would do more than scorch his sorry ass if that happened. They were on a tight schedule, and every man had to execute to the second.

"Hi, there," the girl said more hesitantly. "Lovely day, isn't it?"

The man only nodded. He did not trust his English, though that hardly mattered. Tourists from all over the world came to the Pacific Northwest, and many vacationed to the east in Idaho. He had been told this for his cover.

"You see anybody else out here? In the last hour or so?" The boy came forward, staying a step or two ahead of his girlfriend as if he might be afraid someone would spirit her away.

"No one." The man went cold inside. Were there others here to slow him and further delay the execution of his mission?

"Good. We were hoping we'd find a spot to, you know, sit and talk."

"Oh, Jerry," the girl said, punching him playfully. "That's not what you said you wanted to do." She stood on tiptoe and whispered in his ear. The boy grinned crookedly. The man had a good idea what she had said. She was a typical looking American teenager. Too much meat on her bones, though after the skinny women in his country, he did not mind that so much. But she tittered and appeared pushy. He did not like that in American women. Even the ones he did not spend the night with.

"What's all that in your pack? Looks like rolls of toothpaste." The boy came closer, frowning as he studied the contents of the pack. "Thought you were getting ready to cook some lunch. But I've never seen anything like—"

He got no farther in his examination of the explosives. The man in camo moved swiftly. Two steps took him behind the boy. A brawny arm circled the neck and lifted up a stubbled chin to expose a vulnerable throat. The quick slash sent blood spewing outward in a bright arterial spray.

The move was so practiced and easy that the girl didn't realize her boyfriend was dead before she, too, was killed. The knife slid under her rib cage and angled upward as the man grabbed her Radiohead T-shirt and pulled her forward to prevent her escaping his blade. A tiny gasp escaped her lips, followed by a touch of pink froth and then death. He stepped away as she dropped to her knees and finally fell facedown onto the ground.

He drove his knife blade into the drought-hardened ground to clean it off before he returned it to the sheath at the small of his back. Cursing in three languages but sticking with French for the worst of his rant, he unwound the det cord and strung it along the edge of the trees. When he drew out the full ten yards, he placed a detonator cap on the end and carefully attached wires to it. He retreated to where he had begun and placed the thin wire leads on the ground. He repeated the procedure, going along the edge of the forest in the other direction and placed a second detonator. He ran hard to get back to the juncture of the two lines of explosives and fastened the wires to a small receiver.

He had barely finished screwing down the leads to the radio receiver when his earbud crackled with three short, staccato bursts to alert him.

"Red Leader to Red Two, report."

He swallowed and wiped sweat from his face.

"Red Two here, good to go," he said.

"Fifteen minutes." That was all Red Leader said. That was all the time he had to clear out before the explosives detonated along a twenty-yard stretch of forest. The meadow would allow plenty of oxygen to flow in to feed the fire as it moved deeper into the Boise National Forest, feeding off dead undergrowth and dried trees. Within minutes a hundred hectares would be ablaze.

He slung his now-lightened pack onto his back and loped across the meadow in the direction from which the two young lovers had come. He never broke stride as he stepped over their bodies along the way.

RED LEADER PUSHED the night-vision goggles higher on his forehead. It was late afternoon on a summer day. If he used the NVG in the daylight, he would have been blinded by the full sun, but in a few minutes they would be quite useful to him. He moved around the fire tower at the western edge of the Sawtooth National Recreation Area, taking care to step over the body of the dead forest ranger. A single shot to the forehead had dispatched an unwanted witness.

Red Leader gave no thought to the dead man, because it was his fault he had died. He was supposed to be out on a road doing a fire danger appraisal. For whatever reason, possibly the typical American laziness, he had returned to the fire tower and found a trespasser had broken in.

Red Leader looked at the PDA and chafed at the delay. The mission was running late by almost five minutes. "Red One, come in."

"Red One, aye," came the whisper over the radio. The voice was almost lost in a sea of static. The dry conditions caused interference.

"Are you done?"

"Red Leader, almost finished. Got the det cord strung a bit deeper into the forest than I intended."

Red Leader looked at the small dot moving on his PDA map display. Red One had gone deeper into the Salmon-Challis National Forest to the east than necessary. That threw off the timetable.

His thumb worked the tiny keyboard until a regional weather report slowly scrolled on the screen. The isobars showed the air pressure. The lines squeezed together, indicating mounting wind to the east.

"Are you done, Red One?"

"All done, Red Leader," came the smug reply.

Red Leader pressed another button on the PDA. The Salmon-Challis National Forest erupted in a fireball that sent flames blasting a hundred feet into the air. Red One should have been on time. Red Leader pressed another button and started the timer. The emergency response to this fire would be imminent. Minutes.

Even as his timer hit ninety seconds, the ranger's radio crackled with warnings and orders to call out firefighters.

Red Leader let the fire burn for another eight-and-a-half minutes before triggering the explosives laid by Red Two. All the emergency response in the area was en route to the Salmon-Challis blaze. The fire on the edge of the Boise Basin would be ignored for the time being, since it was smaller in scope.

Smaller but more important. He snapped his head down and brought the infrared goggles over his eyes, squinting as he adjusted the intensity. Even then, blocking out most of the daylight, he saw a wall of intense dancing light. Red Two's fire burned exactly as they had planned. Heavy smoke from the underbrush would lay a pall over the lower lying countryside as the fire worked its way toward Shepard Peak. Except in extraordinary cases, fires were predictable. They burned upward.

Up the side of the mountain and away from the scene of the real action.

"Blue Leader, you have cover," Red Leader said. His radio crackled. The burgeoning fires caused even more static interference.

"Moving in now, Red Leader. Rendezvous in three hours. Mark."

"Red Leader to Blue Leader, out."

He turned off his radio and reset his stopwatch. Three hours to the second. The carefully planned raid proceeded as flawlessly as it had so many times before. He stepped back over the annoying corpse drawing flies in the small lookout tower and spiraled down the stairs, taking them three at a time in his hurry. There was little enough time to skirt the fires his team had set and reach the rendezvous where the real backbreaking work would begin.

No matter where Mack Bolan looked, fire devoured the land. Trees exploded hundreds of feet below him, sending fiery sap close to the V-22 Osprey's rotors. Looking out over the Idaho forest convinced him that nothing could survive down there. The fire was too intense and spread like…a wildfire.

"Where you want to land?" The voice in his headphones might have been either the pilot or the copilot. Bolan couldn't be sure, and it really didn't matter. It took both men's skill at the controls to keep the tilt-rotor aircraft from being buffeted to pieces in the fierce superheated air currents caused by the fire.

"Not down there," Bolan said. His keen eyes studied the raging inferno and found nothing. No landing zone was possible when the very earth itself appeared to be on fire. Besides, Salmon-Challis National Forest was not the spot he was most interested in. It might have been the first place to be torched, but he found the other side of the spiny ridge more interesting. More than his gut feeling, the powers that be back at Stony Man Farm agreed. The real evidence of who set the fires was not here but over near Shepard Peak.

"We're running low on fuel, sir."

This time Bolan knew who spoke. The pilot leaned back and looked over his shoulder at his unexpected passenger. Bolan had been high up in the Rockies north of Leadville at the end of a mission when Aaron "the Bear" Kurtzman had contacted him. Bolan had been looking forward to a much-needed break, possibly taking time to climb Mount Elbert for the solitude it offered and, for a while, simply not worry about someone shooting him in the back.

The V-22 had been dispatched from the 58th Special Operations Wing at Kirtland AFB in Albuquerque, New Mexico, to pick him up. The altitude near Leadville made helicopters unstable to operate, and the V-22 afforded a quick method of transport. For all the fly-by-wire technology involved in the vertical-takeoff-and-landing aircraft, Bolan was more interested in speed. It duplicated the helicopter's vertical capability and added an airplane's range and ability to move him to his target at more than three hundred miles per hour.

"Head due west," Bolan said.

"The other fire?"

Bolan nodded and the pilot went back to his controls. The Osprey banked sharply, giving Bolan another look at the devastation below. Kurtzman had sent a video taken by a commercial airline pilot who had happened to be above the forest when it erupted in flame. Careful examination of the low-resolution video by the Stony Man analysts had given a chilling view of the first seconds of the fire. Bolan recognized the sudden wall of flame for what it was: detonation of a long string of explosives, probably dat cord. The second fire had erupted almost exactly ten minutes later, showing coordination and intent.

The charred stench made his nose wrinkle as he leaned out the doorway and peered down. Intense heat like a mile-long blast furnace seared his face, but Bolan saw only the courage of the firefighters below risking their lives to keep the fire from spreading and devouring more untold square miles of the tinder-dry forest.

"Sir, we're here," the pilot said. Bolan tapped his earpiece. The static interference almost deafened him. "But we got a problem. We can't land down there."

Bolan saw the problem immediately. The fire west of

Shepard Peak had devoured too much of the forest for him to get into the spot where he believed the second, more important fire had been set.

"We could get down, but we might never get back into the air. I'm not risking a seventy-million-dollar aircraft, even if the SecDef himself ordered me down."

Bolan knew the pilot held some resentment toward him personally for being sent on this mission. The orders had come down fast from on high to deliver a single passenger of unknown affiliation to the middle of a forest fire.

"What's your operational ceiling?"

"Twenty-six thousand."

"Take me up to fifteen, then you can go home."

The engines changed pitch as the pilot started an upward spiral. Bolan began getting into his gear. He had to hand it to Kurtzman. The man had anticipated everything. The parachute included with the pack on board when he rendezvoused with the V-22 was exactly what he needed.

"What do you want me to do?"

The pilot's words spilled from the earpiece dropped onto the deck. Bolan was already out the door and tumbling through the turbulent air above the Boise National Forest. He got a good look at the terrain and how the fire had burned from the obvious line where the blaze had started. It looked as if someone had taken a fiery razor to the ground.

More det cord.

Turning slowly as he fell though the heated air, Bolan arrowed his way toward the seared meadow just to the west of the first ignition point. When he was only five hundred feet from the ground—definitely HALO to avoid the worst of the heated updrafts—he pulled the rip cord. The jerk as the parachute deployed caused his teeth to clack together. Then he hit the ground hard. His knees bent and he rolled in the blackened grass, tangling in the shroud lines as they collapsed rapidly.

He finally scraped to a halt and got to his feet. A few minutes later, Bolan had the parachute gathered and weighted down under a rock so it wouldn't blow around in the hot wind all around him.

It was time for the Executioner to go to work.

Stony Man Farm, Virginia

AARON KURTZMAN LOOKED up from his computer console to see the mission controller, Barbara Price, standing in the doorway. The dark circles under her eyes told him she hadn't slept much in days. She said nothing and didn't have to. Kurtzman felt the weight of her unspoken question.

"Nothing yet," Kurtzman said. "Striker has just dropped into the Boise Basin and is doing a quick recon."

"Have you filled him in?"

"I'm still gathering intel," Kurtzman said, glancing at his screen. He looked back up. "What more can you tell me?"

"Not much more," she admitted, heaving a deep sigh. "It seems more and more like an outright attack on the U.S. economy. All the gold was earmarked for delivery to the government to bolster the dollar on world markets. There's no doubt that the last attack was done by a PMC."

"Identified?"

Price shook her head and looked even grimmer.

"How many private military companies can there be on the loose within U.S. borders?" Kurtzman asked aloud, but he didn't expect a response. The question was rhetorical because no one could answer, and they both knew it. The homegrown paramilitary militias had died down over the past few years as government activity against terror cells escalated. This was not the atmosphere a paranoid, super-secret paramilitary group could thrive in. When they were ignored, they flourished in backwoods and the mountains where no one had cared if they blew up old cars with RPGs or shot cutouts of their particular bogeyman. With air travelers having to take off their shoes to check for explosives and everyone jumpy over the slightest thing amiss, the paramilitaries had come under such governmental scrutiny that they could almost be written off.

But not the PMCs. The government used them for security in Iraq and other hot spots around the world. That was fine. What wasn't fine were the PMCs employed by fat cats as bodyguards and even by dictators as personal armies. Most of the PMCs contained mercenaries honed to a keen edge in a dozen different armies worldwide. The various Special Forces branches of the United States supplied their share, but so did the Russian Spetsnaz, the British SAS and all the other European countries with their super-secret, always denied special ops forces. Kurtzman didn't even want to think about the disaffected mercenaries operating out of South Africa, Europe and elsewhere. Too many men and women around the world sold themselves to the highest bidder.

"The last two strikes accounted for well over fifty million dollars in gold," Price said. "That much gold weighs close to two tons. The M.O.s match what's going down in Idaho. I hope Striker can get on their asses in a hurry. We've got to stop them before they bankrupt the country."

Kurtzman felt a shiver travel up and down his spine. Forest fires were set to divert authorities. The PMC strike team had moved into mines with smelters on-site and killed anyone who had not been evacuated. Then the gold had simply vanished. Tons of it. Gone. Like so much golden smoke.

He touched a screen to get a news ticker scrolling slowly along the bottom and smiled without humor. "Gold just hit nine hundred dollars an ounce today, and it's still going up. They're making money even after they steal the bullion. You've got to wonder how they transport that much."

"The question I can't get a handle on is why they need so much," Price said.

Kurtzman felt a little colder. Greed was one thing, but this transcended mere avarice. Whoever was responsible for the thefts was amassing enough cold, hard currency to fund a revolution. A big one.

He opened communication with Bolan to get an update.

"Striker, it's Bear. Report."

"TWO BODIES," Bolan told Kurtzman. "Both murdered." He lightly prodded the man's head with his feet and saw how the spinal cord had been almost severed with a savage slash. The charred corpse revealed little else. The female with him was harder to evaluate, but Bolan wasted no time figuring it out. She was dead and probably by the same hand. He thought she had been knifed in the belly and then the point driven upward into her heart. Bowels, lungs and heart were cinders, but her head remained firmly affixed to her spine. A murder-suicide was out of the question, since there wasn't a knife anywhere to be seen.

Kill the man, then the woman. That was how the solitary killer had moved. Professional. Very professional.

"What do you see at the edge of the forest?"

Bolan's stride lengthened as he went to the worst of the burned area along the meadow. The fire had ravaged the terrain and had moved a mile farther east, where it still roared uphill with voracious intensity. It took only a couple minutes for him to find what remained of one detonator cap and the radio unit that had set off the explosive. He rubbed his fingers over the ground but came up with only soot. Any of the grainy PETN likely used would be completely oxidized.

"He knew what he was doing," Bolan said.

"Latest intel says there is an African PMC on the prowl. We're pinging the CIA and FBI for info on them now to get a better identification."

"That's a mighty big continent."

Kurtzman did not respond, and Bolan hadn't expected him to. He ended the call and pulled out his map and oriented himself, then set off running downhill in the direction of the Lucky Nugget Mine, reaching the tall cyclone fence around the property in under a half hour. He took slow, deep breaths and calmed his pounding heart. Having been at altitude in the Rockies for the prior week helped, but the thin Idaho air still took its toll on him.

As he rested, hands on knees, he looked around the mine site. From the dozen signs painted with huge red letters, this property was owned by Lassiter Industries, a multinational conglomerate owning not only gold mines but copper, silver, manganese and every other metal known to man. Rested, he tossed a broken branch against the fence to see if he might get a shock or trigger an alarm. Seeing no response, and hearing only the miles-distant crackle of a forest being destroyed by fire, he scaled the fence, deftly avoiding the barbed wire strands on top, then dropped lightly to the ground inside.

He reached a well-traveled road and saw a couple abandoned trucks. Of the large crew required to work a mine this size, he saw nothing.

Some equipment had been properly shut down, but most had been hastily abandoned. He knew what had happened. Sirens warned of the forest fire. The miners had to evacuate the mine or risk being trapped a half mile underground if the fire swept this way. Those aboveground would work frantically to get the miners to the surface, then they would all jump into trucks and evacuate. The sheriff's department would be sending constant warnings the entire while. The scream of sirens as the firefighters came in would goad the miners into leaving.

Some might even be volunteer firefighters and join the effort. However it happened, they were all absent from the mine.

But the security staff would remain. Not of their own

choosing, but orders would keep them here until the flames came close enough to singe their eyebrows. Bolan jogged to the main gate, which gaped wide. He peered into the glass-windowed guard booth and saw a man slumped on the floor. There was no reason to check his vital signs. The huge hole in the back of the man's head showed where a single shot had taken him out.

Bolan turned from the guard booth and went immediately to the main office building. The double doors were closed. He tugged at one and it came open easily. The panic bar had not properly locked when the last employee had evacuated.

Halfway down the corridor was the sprawled body of a uniformed woman. She had been shot in the back of the head just like the other guard. Bolan moved from room to room. He found three more murdered security guards. Only one had tried to get his weapon free before six shots had punctured his chest. Examining the entry angles of the wounds convinced Bolan that at least three shooters had sighted in on the poor son of a bitch. From what he could tell, the same caliber weapons had ended the man's life. The killers probably used identical model pistols. That would go with the military precision shown in this attack.

Bolan searched the building from top to bottom. Whoever had killed the guards had not looted the offices. Computers remained on desks. No drawers had been pulled out and searched. Obviously valuable display ingots remained in glass cases in the hallways. Since he found no one alive in the rest of the building to give him eyewitness information, he exited to search other parts of the sprawling mine complex.

Like a compass needle finding magnetic north, he was drawn to a large shed nearby. Heavy steel doors that had once been held closed by intricate locks stood open. Reaching down, he drew his Desert Eagle and let the muzzle precede him into the well-lit interior. Vaults along the walls were open and empty.

The guards positioned at all four upper corners of the building on catwalks had been shot. From the look of it, they had put up a fierce fight but had been overwhelmed by superior firepower.

Walking into the empty expanse in the middle of the building, Bolan saw where a truck had stood next to a loading dock. It took no effort for him to imagine a half-dozen men swarming into the vaults, removing the gold and loading it into the truck before driving away with their valuable cargo.

He had only one more bit of intel to gather. It was surprisingly easy to find the manifests for each of the looted vaults. He kept a running inventory in his head as he read the numbers.

When he finished the tally he stood and stared out the doors where the truck had left.

Three-quarters of a ton of gold stolen. Fifteen thousand pounds. Well over ten million dollars.

His strides long and determined, Bolan left the building, found a car that could be hot-wired easily and roared off in pursuit of the thieves. They couldn't be more than a few hours ahead of him. With that much of a load on the narrow, winding road leading down into Boise, they wouldn't be able to match his breakneck pace.

2

The Executioner drove expertly and far too fast for the narrow gravel road. The mining company had maintained the road well, but hitting ninety in the straightaways and only dropping to sixty in the sharp turns took its toll on his acquired car. Every turn left that much more rubber behind and caused an increasingly uneven ride. Before long the punishment he dished out to the car caused the engine to begin sputtering.

He let up on the gas just a little when he saw an eighteen-wheeler lumbering along ahead. He was still miles outside Boise, and a quick mental calculation of the distance traveled told him this could be the stolen gold. Using the engine compression to brake, he took his foot off the accelerator and coasted into a slot directly behind the truck so that he ran in its blind spot only inches away from the bumper. The driver would have seen him approaching and by now had to know something was wrong. If he slammed on the brakes, Bolan would have to act instantly.

Such a sudden stop was what he expected. That was what he would do to try to get rid of the annoying tail he presented if the roles were reversed. But the driver tapped his brakes, sounded his horn and began slowing gradually. Suspecting a trap, the Executioner followed suit until both truck and car were at a dead stop.

He slid the .50-caliber pistol from its holster and got out of the car. Holding the heavy Desert Eagle at his side, he edged around cautiously. The truck driver had already exited the cab, looking madder than hell.

"What do you think you're doing? This ain't a demolition derby!"

The man waved his arms around like a windmill. Bolan didn't see a weapon but recognized the tactic as a diversion. He ducked away, looked under the eighteen-wheeler but saw no one trying to sneak up on him from the other side. He did hear muffled noises from inside the truck.

Whirling back, he lifted his pistol. The sight of the huge bore pointed in his direction caused the driver to gasp. His mouth dropped open. He tried to speak but no words came out, and his flailing arms stopped their wild motion as he held them high above his head.

"What's in the back?"

"I...you a cop?"

"Open it."

The driver swallowed hard and shuffled around, keeping an eye on Bolan and the pistol in his hand. With his fist he banged twice on the door and yelled, "Mr. Kersey, I'm openin' up." The driver lifted the locking rod and stepped away when the door swung open.

Bolan was prepared for a hail of bullets. He was not expecting a man and several frightened women looking out.

"What's going on?"

"Mr. Kersey, he drove up behind and stopped me and stuck that gun in my face and—"

"Shut up." Bolan wanted answers. "Why are you in the rear of a semi?"

"Are you some kind of police officer?"

"I'm asking, you're answering."

"Well, put that damn thing down. My name's Jerome

Kersey and I'm the superintendent of the Lucky Nugget Mine. I work for Lassiter Industries and—"

"You're all employees?"

"Who'd you think we were? You ordered us to evacuate, and my staff and I were the last ones out. We had to get into this semi because you said the roads were clogged and didn't want a lot of cars adding to the traffic jam. You *are* from the State Police, right?"

Jerome Kersey looked around and frowned when he didn't see any marked patrol cars.

"What's going on? I did what you people asked, and now you're pointing a gun at me!"

"Who told you to evacuate?"

"The state police."

Bolan's mind worked fast. He saw the huddle of men and women behind the mine supervisor and knew these weren't gold thieves. There was no point in asking for ID.

"Sorry about this," he said, holstering his pistol. "Were you told to ship out the gold bullion from the mine?"

"No, of course not," Kersey said. "That was all locked in the storage vaults." Then his eyes narrowed as he looked hard at Bolan. "What are you saying?"

Bolan motioned him out of the truck and to one side where they wouldn't be overheard. He gave the man a quick once-over and saw no suspicious bulges where a gun might be hidden or a knife sheathed.

"I don't have much time, so listen carefully and answer fully," Bolan said. Kersey started to protest. He was in charge of hundreds of employees and was used to giving orders, not taking them. The look on his tall, dark-haired interrogator's face shut him up. He nodded once.

"The security guards left at the mine are all dead."

"Dead?"

"The gold has been removed from the storage vaults. I estimate about three-quarters of a ton was taken."

"I don't have the exact figures, but that would be close." Kersey had gone white with shock at realizing the magnitude of his loss. Bolan doubted his reaction was from hearing that his guards were dead. The theft of all the gold would be a career-ending event. "Who did it?"

"I'm trying to find out. How long have you been away from the mine?"

"Thirty minutes, maybe a little longer."

This surprised Bolan. The gold thieves were even more expert than he had thought. Kersey and his staff had barely left the mine before the thieves had moved in. With this new information for his timeline, Bolan doubted killing the guards had taken more than five minutes. That meant the thieves had loaded just shy of a ton of gold and transported it before he had arrived. The slice of time allotted had been enough for them to vanish into thin air.

"Did you hear or see any helicopters?"

"Of course I did. Observation planes all over. Some heavy-lifter choppers with fire retardant or water or whatever the hell they use to put out fires. They're all over the sky."

Bolan considered this and discarded an airlift being the method of removing the gold. Every plane would be tracked closely by air controllers directing the slurry bombers to the fire. Any unauthorized plane would be spotted instantly. And Kurtzman had not mentioned any, so there weren't any.

"This is an incredible gold mining region. More than three million ounces have been extracted since the mine opened," Kersey said. "You're kidding about my gold being taken out of the vaults, aren't you?"

"One large truck would carry it all," Bolan said. "I didn't pass such a truck. Yours was the first vehicle of any kind I saw on the road. Are there other roads leading away from the mine?"

Kersey shook his head. Bolan had studied the map and not seen any.

"The entire Boise Basin is filthy with gold," Kersey went on. He was beginning to ramble. "Centerville, Idaho City and—"

"What about logging roads?"

"This is a national forest. There's no logging allowed. They hardly allow the railroad crews in and the trains are all diesel electric."

Bolan had heard enough. He slid behind the wheel of his stolen car and wheeled around, kicking up a cloud of dust as he roared back in the direction of the mine. There had been a side road, but he had ignored it because it didn't go anywhere but to the railroad tracks running near the mine. For whatever reason, Lassiter Industries had not run a spur line to bring in supplies and ship out gold. But the railroad was still close enough to make that a viable method of getting away with almost a ton of gold.

The dirt road came up on him fast. He stomped on the brakes, swerved the sedan around ninety degrees and lined up with the rutted lanes. Accelerating onto the rocky road, the car bounced around, sending him lurching back and forth in the driver's seat. Bolan gritted his teeth and drove into the forest. These trees had somehow escaped the fire. As he drove, he appreciated the genius of the robbery even more. The fire had been set to go up the hills and away from this area. Sparks might have ignited the dry underbrush here, but the prevailing winds had made sure that hadn't happened. Bolan wondered what contingency plan the gold thieves had if this part of the forest had been turned into a blast furnace like the rest of the timberlands.

He skidded around a tight curve and crashed head-on into a truck. He had an instant to brace for the crash, but the other driver was taken entirely by surprise.

The sounds of tearing metal and breaking glass filled

Bolan's ears as the car crumpled around him, but the shock of the air bag deploying into his chest almost knocked the wind from him. The Executioner rocked back, then pushed the deflated bag away. He was covered with talcum-fine powder lubricant used in the air bag and his chest felt as if an angry giant had tried to stomp him flat. Recovering, he kicked open the car door and dived out.

There were two men in the truck. The driver slumped over the wheel, but the passenger shoved an HK53 out the window and fired. Bolan hit the ground and rolled, coming to a prone position with his pistol ready. The shooter in the truck cursed. In his nervous haste, he had fired on full-auto rather than using three-round bursts and had emptied his magazine at all the places Bolan was not. The Executioner fired a single round through the side of the truck door. His target let out a groan, pushed the door open and fell to the ground where he flopped about in pain.

Bolan rose and sighted in, only to jerk to the side. A slug ripped through the air where his head had been a split second earlier. He landed hard on his side and fired three quick rounds. One went through the truck's windshield. The other two grazed off the now-starred glass. Through the spiderweb of cracked glass, Bolan saw that the driver was now moving. The crash had only stunned him.

The Executioner made a quick decision. He got to his feet and circled the truck until he got to a spot where he saw more movement inside. Bolan fired twice more and completely destroyed the windshield.

"Don't shoot. I surrender. I'm coming out."

Bolan wanted the man alive but knew a trap when he heard it. These men were professionals and did not surrender after a few shots were exchanged.

"Here's my rifle."

A SIG SG-551 short-barreled assault rifle came tumbling

out and landed in a patch of weeds beside the road. Bolan saw that the receiver was partially open. The rifle had fired once and then jammed.

"I'm coming out. Please don't kill me."

Bolan fired the instant he had a decent shot. The man fell from the cab and landed facedown on the ground. He pushed up and turned to face Bolan. The expression on his face was not one of betrayal at the violation of a surrender but one of utter hatred because he had been outwitted. Then the hand grenade he had intended for Bolan exploded beneath him and lifted his body three feet straight up in the air. The lifeless body crashed to the ground.

Swinging around, Bolan trained his Desert Eagle on the first man out of the truck. He cursed. The man had sneaked off. Bolan needed information, and only one of the mercenaries was left alive to tell him what he needed to know.

He ducked low and looked under the bed of the truck. Nothing. Advancing in a crouch, he went to the rear of the truck and chanced a quick look inside. All he saw was a stack of suitcase-sized wooden boxes partially covered with a tarp. No one could hide under that. Wherever the passenger had gone, it wasn't to get into the truck to die. Bolan ejected the magazine in his pistol and reloaded. He wanted a full clip when he found his man.

A quick glance showed how his target had rolled into a shallow ditch alongside the road and then crawled away fast. The Executioner's quarry had reached a small stand of junipers. Knowing he faced a wounded man who was carrying at least a sidearm and maybe grenades like the driver, Bolan used a large tree as cover. He listened hard but heard nothing moving. The animals in the woods had fallen silent, telling him a human had disturbed them. He listened but heard nothing until a deep inhalation told him where to look. Then he caught the scent of sweat, blood and something unpleasant—cooked flesh.

He slipped around the tree and looked up. Partially hidden ten feet up among the foliage of an oak tree limb lay his camo-dressed prey. Bolan fired three times. The heavy .50-caliber slugs ripped enough wood away from the limb to bring it down. Amid the foliage the stunned man stirred and tried to get away. Bolan fired again but just missed and then had to dodge behind the juniper as the merc fired wildly in his direction.

Bolan took no pleasure at being right about how the man was armed. He had a job to do and was taking too long. All the gunfire would attract the rest of the gang. Judging from the ease with which they had moved through the Lucky Nugget Mine complex, he estimated at least ten had taken part in the operation. Added to the ones in the field setting the fires, he might face twice that if he let them home in on him.

"Who are you working for?" Bolan called out, not expecting an answer.

To his surprise, he garnered a heartfelt "Go to hell."

The accent was faintly European, but Bolan doubted the man had learned English as his second or even third language.

"Africa? South Africa? Afrikaans?"

Bolan wanted to fix his location in the man's thoughts by calling out all the inane questions. He scaled the tree and kept climbing until he came to a limb strong enough to support him. Bolan slithered out on it like a snake and then trained his weapon on the man below where he struggled to get away from the bullet-riddled tree limb.

His finger drew back smoothly as he squeezed off the shot. The heavy slug tore through the mercenary's right shoulder, driving him flat onto the ground. His right arm twitched as he tried to lift his pistol. As he reached over with his left hand, he froze. His head came up and he looked down the barrel of Bolan's Desert Eagle.

"Don't," was all Bolan had to say. The man collapsed and lay on the ground, seemingly beaten. Remembering how the driver had been so contrary, Bolan kicked the pistol away from the man's hand, patted him down and then grabbed his broad belt and heaved. He tossed the man a few feet away, waiting for a hand-grenade detonation.

Nothing.

"Who do you work for?"

"The highest bidder," the mercenary said. He struggled to raise his body off the ground. His left hand pressed into his belly as if he needed the support to hold in his guts, then he painfully sat up. "Just like you," he grated out.

"Who do you think I work for?"

The mercenary tried to shrug, but the bullet he had taken to his right shoulder caused him to blanch in pain instead.

"Same as me. Highest bidder."

"Where's the gold?"

The man laughed harshly and turned his head. Bolan read more into the man's quick glance to the right than he did in the words. The mercenary rubbed his left hand along his belly.

"Where were you going in the truck?"

"Going to blow it up. No evidence." The man lifted his left hand. Bolan fired a round through the man's head but not before a weak, determined finger pressed the button on a small radio detonator he had retrieved from some hidden pouch. The ground shook so hard it made Bolan think he'd gotten caught in an earthquake. Then the door opened on the blast furnace, and fire raced toward him from the direction of the truck. It had been wired as a gigantic firebomb intended to cover the mercenaries' tracks.

Instead, it had given birth to a new forest fire that threatened to devour the Executioner.

The heat threatened to boil the flesh from Bolan's face. Throwing his arm up to protect his eyes, he saw the worst had happened. The mercenaries had been driving back to the junction of the main road to blow up the truck. The resulting fire would cover their tracks completely.

He had to admit their scheme had almost worked—and it had almost killed him. If he had not pursued the mercenary he had blown out of the tree so aggressively, he might have been near their truck when it blew. As it was, though, he couldn't get to his car to escape. Through the wall of scorching-hot flame, he saw the paint on the car he had stolen begin to blister. Then the entire car erupted in a secondary explosion as the flames reached the gas tank.

Bolan headed deeper into the forest. His flesh tingled from the heat. If he didn't put some miles between himself and the fire, he would be charbroiled in only a few minutes. He fell into a distance-devouring jog that carried him along the dirt road toward wherever the mercenaries had come from. As fast as he was, as determined to escape the fire as he could be, the conflagration crept closer and began to warm his back. He put his head down and put on a little more speed, shifting his gait from a jog to a run.

It did no good. The inferno behind him filled the sky with burning sparks that cascaded over the landscape for hundreds of yards. Even sucking smoky air into his burning lungs, Bolan covered a mile in a little over five minutes. And he still wasn't far enough away to feel safe. It was as if the fire toyed with him, letting him get a little farther toward safety before roaring to catch up and spit burning embers onto his clothing. Thinking to veer away from the fire at an angle, he turned off the road and found the dry undergrowth ablaze. He cut back to the road, hoping to go in the other direction, but found it similarly blocked.

He realized these excursions to either side of the road only wasted time and let the fire surge closer, so he continued along the road, eyes watering and lungs screaming from the acrid smoke. Bolan hoped to find out why the mercenaries had come this way but saw no trace of them or what they had been up to.

Running through the smoke-filled air was making it difficult to breathe. The atmosphere looked like L.A. on a smog-alert day and tasted like the inside of a barbecue pit. Over the loud crackling of fire dogging his every step, he heard the whup-whup of a chopper overhead. Bursting into a small clearing, he saw the small helicopter and waved.

The pilot saw him and came lower, buffeted by strong ground winds kicked up by the fire. Landing was out of the question because takeoff would be impossible. The pilot gestured frantically, pointing to a spot away from the road, then he gunned the engine, rose vertically and beat a hasty retreat.

Bolan wished the pilot had tried for the pickup. No guts, no glory, but the pilot was not a military flyer, and Bolan could not hold his caution against him. It just made his own evacuation more difficult, but the only chance he had was to trust the pilot's judgment...even if the man might be one of the mercs who had stolen the gold.

The idea died almost as it formed in his head as a working hypothesis. If he had been another of the force that had robbed the gold mine, all the pilot needed to do was leave. Bolan would stumble about until the fire eventually overtook him—unless he was actually on his way clear of the fire. Knowing the danger of analysis paralysis, Bolan lowered his head and, putting every ounce of energy into the run, headed in the direction the pilot indicated. He burst into another clearing before he realized he was leaving a heavily wooded patch and saw a half-dozen firefighters setting up a small camp. Dressed in their bright yellow fire-retardant gear and respirators, they looked like creatures from another planet.

One turned and pushed up his face mask, letting his oxygen line drape down, so he could shout, "What the hell are you doing here?"

"Had a car wreck."

"You from the mine?" The man gave Bolan a quick once-over and dismissed him as an idiot who let himself get caught by staying too long after the evacuation warning had been issued.

"Just out for a drive when the fire cut me off from the main road."

"That fire was set," the firefighter said. He looked more intently at Bolan. The Executioner did not have to be a mind-reader to know the firefighter thought Bolan might have set the new fire.

"Something exploded behind me. A truck," Bolan said. "The fire's coming this way fast."

"We know." The firefighter turned to glance at a laptop showing an aerial view of the area. Bolan got his bearings and realized how lucky he had been sticking to the road in his escape. If he had veered to either side of the road for long, he would be fried by now. The detonation had sent out flames in a V pattern.

"Get him out of here," ordered another firefighter with three bright orange stripes circling the arms of his yellow fire suit.

"You in charge?"

"I don't know who you are, but a helo recon pilot just reported you were trying to get away. Said he saw a blown-up truck and a car in the middle of where the fire originated."

"My car," Bolan said.

"Buck, get this guy out of here. We don't have time to worry about civilians. We gotta clear as much brush as we can to slow the advance, and we're running out of time."

The one who had spoken initially reached out and took Bolan's arm.

"You heard the man. We go. You stay out of the fire, and I get to come back and do my job." The bitterness in Buck's voice told the story. He was a dedicated firefighter, and Bolan took him away from his job.

"Point me in the right direction. I can find my way out."

This easy way out appealed to Buck. He rubbed his lips with a gloved hand, made a face, then inclined his head toward the far side of the clearing.

"I'll get you on a trail leading downhill to the command station. Masterson only told me to get you out of danger. He didn't say anything about nursemaiding you all the way into Boise." He pointed and started walking clumsily as he fumbled with the dangling respirator.

"You want to stay in your rig?"

"Takes forever to get it on and take it off. Just don't go too fast for me to keep up."

Bolan and Buck walked side-by-side toward the far edge of the clearing. Bolan turned around once to see the towering flames a quarter mile behind. The fire spread faster as it found more dried underbrush. The treetops were exploding with a sound like distant bombs.

"The crowns of the trees are catching fire," Buck said, obviously worried. "That's bad. The fire spreads faster jumping from treetop to treetop than when it burns along the ground."

"You see anybody in the area?" the Executioner asked.

Buck stopped and stared at him. Bolan was sure the firefighter saw the butt of the Desert Eagle in its shoulder holster under his left armpit but said nothing about it.

"Just other firefighters. Two of us have already gotten caught by it." He saw Bolan's expression and explained. "The fire. It's like some wild, uncontrollable beast. Two friends of mine were treated for smoke inhalation and are on the way to the hospital. More of us will join them before it's over, since this fire covers such a wide area."

"Arson," Bolan said. "I caught two of the firebugs, but they got away."

"You a cop? FBI?"

Bolan had no problem verifying that if it helped him find out more from the firefighter. Stony Man Farm specialized in counterterrorism, and setting such fires counted as terrorism, but the mercenaries he had already brought down only used the forest fires to cover their tracks. Gold theft was their primary mission in spite of the havoc they created.

"Homeland Security," he said, which was close enough to the truth to be believable.

"You're doing a piss-poor job of policing the borders," the firefighter said unexpectedly.

"One job at a time."

"Yeah, look, keep going in this direction. You'll reach a creek. Follow that downstream until you see our base camp. There's a couple hundred people there, so it's hard to miss."

Buck started back to his crew to fight the fire, but his radio crackled and the frightened voice sounding from it caused him to grab it frantically.

"Come in, Masterson. Repeat. Repeat. What's your report?"

"Your team got caught and is surrounded by the fire," Bolan said. He had experience enough to decipher almost any message coming through intense static and dropping words.

"Go, get out of here," the firefighter said. He worked at the walkie-talkie but got no response.

"I can help. You can't do anything by yourself."

"I can get to them. We have to evac now."

"It'll be with casualties," Bolan said. He had a mission to complete, but he wasn't going to let Buck try to save the others in his crew alone. That would only add one more death to the impressive list of destruction the gold thieves had already racked up.

"They'll chew my ass good for this, but you're right. I need help, and I don't care if you're only a civilian. Come on!"

Two of them doubled the chance of rescuing the trapped firefighters.

"I'll need some equipment in your camp," Bolan pointed out. He did not give the firefighter a chance to argue. Seconds mattered. They retraced their steps, but Buck did not slow when they came to the stacks of equipment. He plunged on toward the wall of smoke masking the edge of the fire zone.

Bolan scooped up a respirator and goggles. The rest of the equipment—fire-retardant jacket, boots and equipment for clearing brush—was meant for the firefighters who would remain close to the blaze for a long time. He wanted only to rescue the men trapped so he joined Buck and immediately regretted not putting on a jacket or a fire helmet. Tiny sparks landed on his arms and in his hair, burning holes and causing distracting pain. But he had put up with worse in his day. He began squashing the tiny fires in his clothing as if swatting mosquitos.

"It moved fast this way. We never saw it coming because the copter pilot said it was following a dirt road, not coming downhill toward us."

"The wind changed direction," Bolan said. He adjusted the face mask and respirator before plunging through the wall of fire. The fierce flames clawed at him like some wild animal, but he burst through and came out in a curiously empty area already burned clean of vegetation. Two of the firefighters were flat on the ground and not moving. Another sat, clutching his leg and uttering curses mostly about the fire. The other two worked to make contact using their walkie-talkies.

"The stream," Bolan shouted, making himself heard over the roar of the fire. "Where is it?"

"We've got fire-resistant blankets. We can weather it. We're only on the edge." Buck did not sound confident. One of the unconscious men was the fire team leader, and there did not seem to be anyone left willing to make independent decisions.

"They won't make it," Bolan said. He rolled over the unconscious fire team leader, then hefted him up over his shoulders in a fireman's carry. Bolan did not wait for the others but headed in the direction Buck had indicated earlier.

He had hardly gone a dozen yards when he found a new wall of fire. Courage had less to do with his action than knowing this was his only chance to survive. Bolan put his head down and charged like a bull. He broke through the dancing flames and came out on the other side. If his luck had not held, he might have found himself in the midst of the raging fire rather than on scorched earth. Weaving through the blackened trees, he headed downhill with his burden and soon found the narrow but deep stream. He dropped his load into the middle of the water. Making sure the unconscious man's head was propped above the surface, Bolan turned and started back to help the rest of the firefighters.

He got only a few yards back uphill when he spotted four men stumbling along.

"Where's Buck?"

The lead firefighter shook his head. He tried to grab Bolan's arm to stop him, but the warrior was not to be deterred so easily. He broke the grip and ran back. The wall of voracious flame he had breached before was gone now, moving on with a speed that amazed him. He swiped at his goggles, removing a thin sheen of soot that had kept him from seeing Buck limping along. The firefighter's right leg refused to bear his weight. If he kept hopping that way, he would never get to safety.

In a flash, Bolan got to the firefighter's side and slipped an arm around him to lend some support.

"You're some kind of madman," Buck grated out. "Nobody's paying you to look after me. Hell, they're not even paying me that much. I'm a volunteer, like the rest of my team."

Bolan steered Buck off at an angle, goaded by the increasing heat at his back. They finally reached the creek and sloshed into it.

"Where're the others? Where are they?"

"Get down into the water," Bolan ordered. He shoved Buck to a sitting position. "They're a bit farther upstream."

"You saved Lee? Lee Masterson?"

Bolan immersed himself in the stream and felt every burn and blister on his body turn to ice as the water washed over him. He still had to use his respirator to breathe, but the fire now ran parallel to the stream.

"We're gonna make it," Buck said. "You saved me."

"You'd have made it on your own."

"Don't be so sure of that. I think my leg's broken from a spill I took. If it turned into a compound break, there's no way I could have made it to safety. Hell, I couldn't have made it to the railroad tracks, much less here."

"Railroad?"

"There's one that runs parallel to the stream, a mile farther downhill," Buck said. "But what good're train tracks? They've cleared the regular traffic just to be on the safe side. I wish we could get supplies sent by train." Buck closed his eyes and choked back his pain. Talking kept his mind off his injury. "Even then, the higher-ups don't like to depend on trains. The heat can actually melt the tracks and warp the rails. Then we'd have a derailment as well as a fire to deal with."

"Clear the traffic? There was a train that came by recently?"

Buck moaned softly as he clutched his leg.

Bolan rummaged through the firefighter's pack and found a morphine syringe. He expertly opened the ampule, then injected the drug directly into the injured leg.

"Burns. Never had a shot like that before."

"You'll get sleepy in a minute. What about the train?"

"Tracks," Buck said in a weak voice. "Don't know th
schedule but the boss said they had to get one out of the wa
'fore we could move in equipment. Equipment. Need…" Buc
drifted off to a troubled sleep, but the pain was bearable fo
him now, thanks to the narcotic.

Bolan made sure Buck's head would remain above th
water, then yelled for the other firefighters. When he saw th
bright yellow jacket with the orange stripes splashing down
stream toward them, he knew Buck would be all right. The fir
team leader had recovered and would provide needed guidanc
for the rest of his men.

Bolan left before the fire team leader reached them to as
questions better left unanswered. He made his way in the di
rection Buck had indicated and saw the railroad tracks.

This was how the mercenaries had gotten the heavy gol
away from the area, with little risk they would be found ou
Where did they ship it? Like a hunting dog on a scent, the Exe
cutioner went to the train tracks and began walking. Hi
mission was just beginning.

The Executioner reached a switching juncture in the railroad tracks. From what he could tell, one went due west toward Oregon and the Pacific coast while the other angled to the southwest. If the mercenaries had loaded their stolen gold onto a train, it could have gone in either direction. It was time for him to get some help.

Bolan fiddled with his satellite phone a bit and finally got a connection to Stony Man Farm. Kurtzman came online immediately.

"Good to hear from you, Striker."

"The gold was trucked to a railroad spur, loaded on a freight car and it's on its way out of Idaho. Did it go west or southwest?"

"We've been looking into this," Kurtzman responded. "All the fires preceding gold thefts were set near rail lines."

"That's how they get the gold away. Where do they take it?"

"We're working on that." Kurtzman sounded distant. Bolan knew he was juggling intel input from a half-dozen different sources. That didn't make waiting any easier. He kept hiking along the tracks, choosing the line going to the southwest for no good reason other than it *felt* right. His survival instincts had been honed to perfection over the years, and he had learned to rely on his gut to find what others couldn't.

"There's a new fire," Kurtzman said.

"I almost got caught in it. They blew up the truck they used to move the gold from the mine to cover their tracks."

"Unless you're in western Nevada watching the forests in

Pine Grove along the California border go up in smoke, we're talking about a different fire."

"What gold mine is near the new fire?"

"The burn started outside the town of Hawthorne. There are two major gold producers there, but only one has a railroad line not owned by the mining company running alongside its property."

"How long has the fire been burning?"

"We got a satellite view almost immediately. Lots of satellite recon resources are being retasked to watch the western states because of this. The fire hasn't been burning longer than a half hour."

"Check the tracks for moving freight trains. Watch for off-loading and determine their destinations."

"It's being done as you speak, Striker. Only one train meets all the criteria," Kurtzman said. "Its destination is Oakland, California. From the manifest, it carries container shipments headed for overseas ports. Made in America."

Bolan said wryly, "Stolen in the U.S. is more like it. I need transport to the Oakland shipyard."

"There's a problem with transport, Striker," Kurtzman said. "The V-22 returned to its home base after you left so precipitously. Everything else is tied up fighting the fires. We can't even get a spec ops team in for another six hours."

"No reason to bring in the cavalry," Bolan said. "The bad guys have already ridden into the sunset." He looked west and knew that was the literal truth. The mercenaries had finished their work and moved on, leaving the forest ablaze around Boise. Trying to catch them near the fires in Nevada was also a fool's errand. He would arrive too late to do anything more than tramp through forests turned to charcoal.

"Striker, we have transport for you, but you'll have to share the ride."

"When and where?" Bolan got his answer, but he didn't like it.

"SO WHO ARE YOU?" the small, wiry lawman demanded, coal-black eyes sharp and hard as they fixed on Bolan. He had a gray mustache waxed to sharp points and sported a ten-gallon cowboy hat with a snakeskin band straight out of some B western. He wore his sidearm in an Old West–style hard leather holster. From where he stood, Bolan could not see the make of the gun but thought it was probably a replica of the old .44 Peacemaker.

"Names don't matter."

"I didn't ask your name. I don't give two hoots and a holler about what you call yourself—or what somebody told you to call yourself. Who *are* you? Not FBI. They come waltzing in, lording it over everybody. First words out of their mouths are 'I'm Special Agent Who Doesn't Give a Shit,' and you're not local. Not with the pressure coming down on me. You can't be CIA. They don't operate inside the country. So, I'll ask again, not quite so polite this time. Who the *hell* are you?"

"I'm the cargo you'll get to Oakland, Marshal Phillips."

"Closemouthed," the U.S. marshal said. For the first time a small smile curled the corners of his mouth. It didn't last long. "You're taking me off my assignment, you know."

Bolan had walked miles and finally had reached a spot where he jumped onto a freight train to ride into Boise. From the rail yards he had gone directly to the U.S. marshals' office, as Kurtzman had told him to do.

"We're on the same team," Bolan simply said.

"A good thing since you're bigger 'n me. Not that I haven't had to deal with that problem most of my life. Danged near everyone's bigger 'n me. I'm only five-foot-eight. Didn't keep me outta the SEALs, though. Never weighed over one-fifty, either."

"Is that with or without the mustache?"

Phillips laughed with some obvious enjoyment at the verbal

riposte. Then his face went hard, and he pushed past Bolan to look into the outer office.

"No time to lollygag, mister. Our ride's ready." As Phillips strode through the office, men and women thrust things into his hands. He glanced at a couple folders and dropped them back onto desks. He kept several others and tucked them under his arm. Bolan followed in his wake, ignored by the deputies. That suited him fine. It gave him a chance to glance at the manila folders Phillips had discarded. All carried the Department of Homeland Security logo and dealt with recent terrorist activities.

Bolan barely settled into the backseat of a standard-issue black SUV with tinted windows as the driver floored it. He was pressed back into the seat beside the marshal.

"Here, read this," Phillips said, passing over the files he had kept after his quick exit from the office. "What more can you tell me about the sons of bitches who set those fires?"

Bolan had started to dismiss the man again but took a closer look at what he had been handed. Two of the files were jackets on the pair he had dispatched before they had blown up the truck. The third file carried a picture of someone he had seen before in a Top Secret file at Stony Man Farm.

"Don't know these two, except I killed both of them. This one's a known commodity. Jacques Lecroix. Did wet work in Algeria for anyone who paid his price. He dropped off the radar screen two years ago."

"You know your PMC recruits, mister." Phillips didn't miss a beat. "Is there anything more current you know about him?"

"He worked for a private military company out of Paris before he disappeared." Bolan worked through all the threads of memory connected to Lecroix. "Africa. That's all I remember. He might have been seen last in South Africa."

"We got a lead on him from some wino along the Boise skid row. Not sure what Lecroix wanted, but it was obvious even to a whiskey-besotted derelict that he was being recruited as cannon fodder. I suspect Lecroix wanted to send a few of Boise's less fortunate into the rail yard to flush out the security."

"He could reconnoiter himself and not leave a trail," Bolan pointed out.

"He was behind schedule, at least that was the impression. If he is hanging out with men like these two—" the marshal tapped the other files "—he's not into finding locals to do the real dirty work for him. One was an explosives expert. The other worked for a PMC in Iraq until six months ago when he upped and disappeared. His boss thought he might have gotten a better offer and just left without giving notice."

Bolan nodded. Allegiances were bought and paid for, and some former employers might not look favorably on anyone leaving their service for a competitor. He scanned Lecroix's file again, trying to piece together the unrelated bits. Chances were good the mercenary had gone to work for a PMC in Africa, since his earlier training had been in the northern tier of the continent. But, as those things went, northern Africa was peaceful enough at the moment. Not more than a few abortive uprisings and rebel attacks that never amounted to anything had been reported in the past couple years. This was hardly the place for an ambitious soldier of fortune like Jacques Lecroix.

He pulled out his satellite phone and called Stony Man. Aaron Kurtzman answered immediately.

"I'm with Marshal Phillips on the way to the airport," Bolan said, letting Kurtzman know he had to watch everything he said. "The marshal has identified the two I killed, along with Jacques Lecroix. What can you tell me about him?"

"The Katanga Swords," came the measured answer.

"I've heard of the group. A PMC," Phillips supplied, making no effort to conceal his eavesdropping. Bolan's estimation of him went up a little. The marshal wasn't into playing games. He knew Bolan expected him to listen to everything said and didn't pretend otherwise.

"Out of the Democratic Republic of the Congo," Kurtzman said. "We're working on more."

Bolan signed off and tucked the phone away. He had thought this mission was a nonstarter at first. Tracking down a firebug who got his rocks off watching trees go up in flame had hardly seemed a reasonable use of his time. Once he had seen the clockwork precision of how the fires had been set and appreciated the scale of the resulting theft, he had been more favorably inclined toward the mission. Learning a mercenary of Lecroix's caliber headed up the operation made this a high-priority item. Lecroix did not come cheap and did not waste his time unless there was a challenge in the mission. He killed as much to relieve boredom as he did to amass great wealth, but more than these casual motives, he appreciated a challenge. A man driven only by greed was vulnerable. Lecroix was more dangerous because he sought out goals other than riches.

What was he looking to do?

"He's not taking the gold for himself. He's been hired to steal it," Bolan said.

"Who needs a mountain of gold?" The way Phillips spoke, he did not expect an answer, but this was a reasonable question. Somebody had hired a top-notch mercenary and his crew to steal hundreds of millions in gold. Who?

The SUV skidded to a halt and Phillips bailed out before the vehicle came to a complete stop. Bolan followed and saw a Gulfstream G550 jet waiting on the runway.

"Private? You must have called in a lot of favors for that," Bolan said.

"Not really. As anxious as our Monsieur Lecroix is to steal the gold, there's someone just as eager to get it back."

Bolan climbed up the narrow steps and ducked to get inside. The corporate logo told the story.

"Is there an actual man named Lassiter behind Lassiter Industries?"

"There surely is. Set yourself down, and be sure to strap in real tight. The takeoff's likely to be abrupt, and I told the pilot to push this puppy to its full .8 Mach."

Bolan had barely fastened his seat belt when the acceleration pushed him into the soft seat cushions. There was no waiting at the end of the runway for takeoff, either. The pilot put the power to the twin engines and sent the corporate jet into a steep climb.

"He flew F-14s off the *USS Ronald Reagan,*" was the only comment Marshal Phillips made.

"THE U.S. MARSHALS' OFFICE seems to have more resources than ever get mentioned in reports," Bolan said. They had landed at the Oakland International Airport where a clone of the other SUV waited for them.

"Amazing what having some dedicated people who make big political contributions can do," Marshal Phillips said. He grinned crookedly. "Truth is, there's a whole lot of folks who want to see the forest fires ended who don't know squat about gold being stolen. And I don't just mean the Sierra Club or Friends of the Forest, either."

Bolan stared out the tinted window as the other cars on the freeway slipped behind them. The driver was expert and kept them moving in and out of the tight knots of traffic that otherwise would have stalled them, getting to the rail yards in record time.

"We're going after the same miscreants, me and you, but for different crimes. I grew up in the forests of Idaho and Montana and hate seeing them turned into charcoal briquettes. That the gold was stolen from under my nose doesn't do a whole lot for my self-esteem, either."

Bolan doubted the sinewy lawman had any problems with self-esteem. No former SEAL did. They knew their abilities and their limitations and worked within them—or beyond them, as the mission required.

"Where do we go?"

Bolan checked the small video screen on his satellite phone. A single number burned there in a muted green.

"Eastern side of the yards. The train's coming in right now. There is a siding for the freight cars we're most interested in."

"Container cars," Phillips said, nodding. "Now how'd they get the gold into a container ready to be shipped overseas so fast?"

"That's a good guess that it's headed out of the country, but it might also be off-loaded and hooked to a truck cab."

Phillips scornfully looked at him. "Now, you don't believe that. I don't, and I'm nothing but a poor ol' hick hayseed marshal from the boondocks."

"Does that work with many people?"

"You'd be surprised. I'm used to dealing with government agents and just fell into the role," Phillips said. "There's the main switching tower. Let us out here."

The marshal was already on the way out of the SUV before the driver hit the brakes. Bolan found himself wondering if the man's SEAL training had consisted of nothing but jumping out of moving vehicles. It was a shame because he was getting to like the marshal, but he knew they would part company soon. Phillips had a limited interest in the gold theft. Bolan wanted the entire picture to come clear—then he would have to act.

They climbed the winding staircase to the top of the switching tower, which looked like a control tower at an airport. Three men sat in front of computer controls while a fourth surveyed the yard through a pair of binoculars.

"You can't come up here," the man with the field glasses said automatically. "This is a restricted area."

Bolan let Phillips do the official "make nice" and dish out all the legalese. He trusted the marshal not to say too much about what they intended to find.

"The cars on the freight train at the edge of the yard," Bolan said to a man working on a computer with a screen like a radar display. "Can you track individual ones?"

"That's how we do it these days," the man said. "Used to be we needed somebody in a caboose to watch. No more cabooses. We hang a computer unit on the last car and monitor the others by RFIDs."

"Does every car have its own radio frequency ID chip?"

"Most all the cargo is individually tagged by the shipper. We don't bother scheduling particular cars. The shipper loads up, and the freight car sits on a siding until a train going in the right direction comes through. It's hooked up, then shuttled around so the car eventually ends up where it is needed. We track by satellite to make certain nothing goes astray—too much—but you could say rail shipments are mostly hit or miss."

"That sounds as if it might take a long time for some cars to get to their destination."

"Right. Freighting by rail isn't a science, not like putting it on a truck and shipping point-to-point. Excuse me." The man began working to switch the tracks and guide the freight cars onto the proper sidings prior to unloading.

Phillips came over and said quietly, "What now?"

The Executioner had carefully observed the computer displays and knew which cars had arrived from Boise by their computer IDs.

"The cargo isn't going to have any of Lecroix's team with it. If they're even still in the country, they're already at the docks waiting for the containers."

"So let's follow the shipment and see how many wharf rats we can scare up."

Bolan couldn't have said it better.

"Is that the railcar?" Marshal Phillips asked, lifting his chin rather than pointing with his finger. He walked softly, making almost no sound as his flashy hand-tooled cowboy boots crunched into the cinders scattered throughout the rail yard.

The Executioner took out his satellite phone and contacted Stony Man Farm about his progress.

"You have the freight car numbers registered?" he asked Aaron Kurtzman. The response was almost immediate.

"No such cars on the inventory," came the unsurprising answer.

"It's about what I suspected. Those cars will disappear, and the railroad company will never know they shipped them." Bolan signed off and tucked his satellite phone into his jacket pocket.

"They must be cheap sons of bitches," Phillips said. "They steal the gold and then ship it at no cost. The port isn't too far away, and there must be a dozen sets of tracks running over there."

"They'll hook their car to a legitimate train," Bolan said. The railcar he had his eye on looked like any other, but it took him a few seconds to figure out why it was different. He felt a little satisfaction seeing that the thieves had made an error. The serial number on the freight car that had come in from Idaho transporting the gold had one digit less than the others from the same company. Lecroix had allowed somebody to do a shoddy job. If an inspector at any spot along the long miles between Oakland and Boise had bothered to check, it would have shown up as a freeloading car.

"The computer chip must read all right," Bolan said. "Otherwise, every time the train passed through a station or yard between here and Idaho it would have been recorded in error."

The Executioner itched to examine the freight car and see if it still held close to a ton of gold, but he refrained. Lecroix might have sent one of his Katanga Swords mercs to keep an eye on it. One wrong step would scare them off. Lecroix was vicious and cunning, but he would jettison millions of dollars worth of the gold rather than jeopardize his entire operation, whatever it was.

This set Bolan to thinking along a different path. He had assumed that he could wrap everything up at the Oakland seaport. Stop the gold, end the mission. He realized this river ran deeper than he had suspected at first, and he had barely gotten his feet wet. Lecroix was accumulating the vast hoard of precious metal for someone else—finding the purpose for such funding only led to another mission.

"That whole line of cars'll be pulled around by that teeny little electric engine," Phillips said. "Might be the engineer knows something."

"Might be he only works for the railroad company."

Phillips pursed his lips and thought a few seconds before saying, "I'm taking the gold back. I want the men responsible for stealing it and setting the fires, but the gold goes back to Idaho with me as evidence."

"Do you work for Lassiter Industries or the government?"

"Same end of the trail this time," Phillips said. "If old man Lassiter is happy not to get ripped off, I'll be happier than a hog in slop bringing the men who set those fires to trial. They were beautiful forests, all gone now, along with some fine men and women."

"How many?"

"We've found the bodies of two rangers, along with a young

couple near the edge of one fire and close to ten guards at the mine. The way these things work, we're likely to find other bodies after the fires are out. We've been lucky that none of the firefighters have died. Oh yeah, the gold's important, but I want the men responsible for the murders."

Bolan doubted that was going to happen. He had not been given specific orders concerning Lecroix, but taking the mercenary alive was unlikely. Lecroix had survived too many coups and outright wars over the long, bloody years for that. As good a lawman as Marshal Phillips might be, he wasn't in the same class as Lecroix or even members of the Katanga Swords.

"We should mark that freight car," Phillips said unexpectedly.

Bolan considered what the marshal had said and knew he was right. He looked around and found a box filled with black spray paint cans. Grabbing two, Bolan ran to the car and took a quick look underneath to be sure he wasn't walking into a hornet's nest. Nobody patrolled the other side of the freight car. He stepped away, surveyed his new metal canvas and sprayed a corner near the door with a triangle pattern. Three more quick swipes left innocuous-appearing marks not likely to be noticed by anyone handling the car.

"You got a lousy sense of tagging," the marshal said. "No flair for it, none at all."

Bolan didn't reply. He stared past Phillips at a man holding a sawed-off shotgun. A long slender rod wrapped in black electrician's tape was thrust in the scruffy man's belt. A thousand things raced through the soldier's head, but one conclusion seemed inescapable. If he made a move for his own pistol the shotgunner would fire and cut Phillips in two.

"You're too old to be gangbangers. Whatcha defacin' property for?" The man with the shotgun moved around. To his credit Phillips had not reacted other than to lift his bushy eyebrows a little. His hands hung at his side, but Bolan saw small muscles tense to prepare him to draw the Colt .44 from his holster.

"You make a move for that gun and you're dead. Both of ya!"

"Put down your weapon," Phillips said. "You're threatening a U.S. Marshal, and that is a federal offense. You could be doing hard time in Leavenworth for it."

"I'm the law around here," the man said, moving around even more to face Phillips. This caused him to shift the muzzle of his shotgun off-line. "I'm the railroad dick and I say—"

Bolan moved like lightning. He kicked out and caught the man's right hand in such a way that the nerves went numb from wrist to shoulder. A second kick knocked the shotgun from the twitching hand. To his surprise, the man was not paralyzed at what had to be real pain in his right arm. He slid the flexible steel rod from his belt and swung it clumsily with his left hand at Bolan's head.

The rod bent over the Executioner's grasping hand, and it felt as if it broke important bones in Bolan's wrist. The Executioner was not even aware of his next move. He spun and drove his left elbow into the back of the railroad detective's head. Without so much as a gasp, the man crumpled to the ground.

Bolan rubbed his wrist and got circulation back into it. A nasty bruise already spread along his forearm, but he ignored it. Nothing had been broken, in spite of the sudden surge of pain that had accompanied the blow.

"Now we got ourselves a problem with him," Phillips said, hardly blinking at all that had happened. "We have to report this, but the car's getting ready to be moved."

"Vibration in the rails," Bolan said, pressing the toe of his boot against the track.

"You catch on fast," Phillips said. His tone was neither sarcastic nor congratulatory. It was a simple statement.

Bolan reached down and grabbed a handful of shirt. He grunted as he pulled the railroad detective along the ground, bouncing him over tracks and finally getting him to a spot behind a tall mechanical track switch where his body wouldn't be seen easily. With the unconscious man taken care of, Bolan looked around and saw the only spot where he could watch without being viewed.

He hopped into an empty freight car on a siding and dropped flat on his belly so he could peer out. Phillips lay prone beside him.

"For a big man, you surely do move fast. Reminds me of my SEAL instructor." Phillips didn't even look at Bolan when as an afterthought, he added, "I hated that man's guts and would have gladly stuck a knife into his belly."

"Why didn't you?"

"He got sent on a mission and didn't come back. The new instructor wasn't any better."

The freight car Bolan had marked with the small black triangles shivered and then began stuttering along the track. An electric engine had hooked onto it and moved the railcar to the end of a long line of other freight cars. More than once Bolan saw the engineer in the electric engine hold up what had to have been a device for reading the computer chip RFIDs marking every car. In less than twenty minutes, the engineer hitched his engine to the front of the freight cars and began moving them along a spur line.

"We lie here watching or do we hitch a ride?"

"We know where they're going," Bolan said. "Let's get to the docks ahead of the cars." He was hesitant about Phillips coming with him. If there was any trouble, the marshal had to line up on the side of the law—and Bolan knew he didn't have time to wait for backup, subpoenas or any of the rest of that paper the legal machinery churned out so slowly.

Phillips looked hard at him, then a slow smile came to his lips.

"I ought to remain here and see to the railroad detective. He might need to go to the hospital for a concussion since you hit him so hard. You go on and scout out the terrain. I'll be long when I can." The marshal held up a set of car keys that Bolan snatched in the blink of an eye.

Bolan shook Phillips's hand and never looked back as he ran to where they had parked the black SUV. Once inside he keyed the ignition and roared off, taking turns with reckless abandon. The Oakland shipyards loaded containers from both trains and semis for shipment all over the world. The place covered more than two square miles and stretched along San Francisco Bay, with an improbable number of docks thrusting out into deeper water.

He parked the SUV and went into the middle of the railroad switching yard. Men using forklifts were unloading the freight cars and flatcars and paid Bolan no attention as he searched for the proper car. He walked to the end of the line of cars he was sure had been brought directly in from the rail yard but did not see the freight car with the gold.

Then he remembered why he had painted the black markings on the car. Several were wet, as if they had been through a rainstorm, even though the bright cloudless California sky ruled that out. Those cars caught his attention when he saw water-based paint dripping off the sides and puddling on the ground. Somewhere between the rail yard and the demarcation here dockside, three freight cars had been hosed down. Whatever fake insignia had been painted on them had been washed off.

But not the spray-painted black triangles near the doors on one. Those had been done recently and by the Executioner using indelible paint.

He stepped back and saw the three cars were being shunted to a different spur. Walking slowly after the cars as they were pulled by a small electric engine, he watched gates across the tracks opening. A half-dozen men, all wearing ponchos, patrolled just behind the chain-link gates. The day was cool but not that chilly for someone used to the Bay area breezes.

One man reached up to give the gate a shove to close behind the three freight cars and lifted his poncho enough t reveal a machine gun slung beneath. From the way the othe walked, Bolan guessed all the guards were armed to the teet This was a high crime area, and theft from the docks coul amount to millions over a month or two. But Bolan kne these particular guards were armed to protect the spoils theft, not prevent it.

The gate slid shut across the railroad tracks and th guards dispersed.

Walking slowly parallel to the fence, he came to a sp where he could study the main office building and the sig painted on it. He nodded to himself. Kurtzman had called i This section of the docks was run by the Democratic Republi of the Congo. It wasn't unusual for foreign companies to ow segments of the dock business or even entire ports.

Bolan considered walking in through the front door of th shipping company, possibly offering a story about shippin cargo to the Congo, but he would have needed papers an some serious money to flash in order to keep the men insid from becoming suspicious. So he strolled on, careful not t appear too interested in the men and women inside the offic or what went on in the loading area near the docks.

He leaned against the chain-link fence and got a good loo at the only docked ship being loaded with cargo container Huge nets swung upward, suspended from powerful crane carrying metal containers to the broad deck of the *Spirit Brazzaville.* Bolan had lost track of the three freight cars, in cluding the one he knew contained the gold stolen in Idaho The buildings blocked a good view of much of the loadin area. With so little weight compared to the huge freighter capacity, the gold could be tucked in a single sea cargo con tainer and then loaded onto the ship in front of his eyes an he would never know it.

Stepping back a pace, he eyed the chain-link fence. He saw small wires running through the links just under the concertina wire looping along the top of the fence. Touching one of those wires would set off alarms all over the dock. Bolan considered his chances getting inside by this route to be close to zero. If it were dark and he had an hour to work, he could get around this system, climb the fence, avoid the razor wire and go exploring along the docks. Waiting for dark was out of the question, since the *Spirit of Brazzaville* looked ready to sail. It might be ready to sail with the morning tide—or even the evening tide. That made it all the more imperative that Bolan verify the gold was aboard and find out the ship's destination.

It might be as easy as going to the harbor master and looking at a manifest, but where the ship ported was of no interest to him. What they did with the stolen gold was.

"I can get a search warrant within the hour."

Bolan shook his head. He had heard the telltale clicking of Marshal Phillips's boots on the pavement as he came up from behind.

"You wouldn't get it soon enough to matter. The ship is ready to set sail."

"I can call in a favor or two from a local federal judge. The Coast Guard might get an anonymous call that there's contraband aboard."

"You're not going to recover the gold that way," Bolan said. "If they reached the open ocean, they would drop overboard anything they didn't want found."

"That's a powerful waste of gold," Phillips pointed out.

"This operation has been set up with great attention to detail. The best mercs available are setting the fires and stealing the gold for someone with a real need for it." Bolan's quick eyes worked along the fence and back to the main office.

"The gold's evidence. It's my sworn duty to recover it, especially if it is going to be taken out of my jurisdiction."

"That's likely considered sovereign territory on the other side of this fence. To break in there would the same as invading a foreign country, with you wearing that U.S. Marshal's badge."

"I am an officer of the United States government," Phillips said, nodding as he twirled his mustaches.

"I'm not," Bolan said, the plan forming in his head.

"Didn't think any service would own up to you working for them," the marshal said. "What do you want me to do?"

"Give up hope of getting the gold back," Bolan said. "Then I want you to follow my orders exactly."

The Executioner began outlining what he expected of the marshal.

"Report, Red Leader," Jacques Lecroix said, his voice low as he held the cell phone close to his lips. He looked over at the tall, stately woman, sleekly dressed in a muted pastel designer suit that fit her perfectly and contrasted with her chocolate skin. Seemingly bored, she stared out into the San Francisco Bay, but Lecroix knew nothing slipped past her. Coraline N'Kruma had shown up unexpectedly at the last moment as he had arrived in Oakland. The only explanation for her appearance was distrust on the part of his employer.

Lecroix cursed under his breath. Everything had gone well, except for the need to sacrifice the fool in Idaho who had failed to set his explosive charges according to schedule. Of all the Katanga Swords, the one dead man had to be politically connected. Lecroix had not wanted to bring him on this job because of his lack of experience in the field, but time had crushed in on them and there had been no choice. Now this lapse in his judgment and leadership came back to threaten him.

As he would not hesitate to remove anyone in the way of completing his mission, so N'Kruma would report anything, no matter how damning.

"Blue Leader, we are three miles out, in heavy traffic on the Nimitz Freeway."

"Understood," Lecroix said.

"Is he the one who killed poor Atta?" N'Kruma never turned from her study of the ships steaming out into the harbor and under the Golden Gate to ports all over the world. As silken as those words were, Lecroix heard the edge.

"He did the right thing. We were on a strict timetable."

"The right thing," she mused. N'Kruma turned and smiled. Lecroix wished she had not. Her small, perfect white teeth reminded him of the fangs of some jungle beast. Not a lion but a tiger or leopard. Her lips pulled back a little more, letting him see what might have been vampire fangs. Lecroix had faced armies and never flinched. He forced himself not to show any emotion now. Any weakness would be immediately reported.

At the thought of how vulnerable he was, his mind slipped away from the unspoken combat between them to the possibility of hijacking the gold waiting to be loaded onto the *Spirit of Brazzaville.* Three entire freight cars had brought the gold to the docks, where it had been reloaded into a single sea container destined for immediate transport. The huge freighter heaved in and out as powerful waves sloshed against its bay side, but with each passing minute that movement damped with load after load of heavy machinery bound for the Orient. The shipping container holding the gold would be the last added to the cargo on the deck so it would be easily guarded.

"Red Leader, continue with dispersal plans."

"Understood, Blue Leader."

"Red Leader, Blue Leader, it is all so...dramatic," N'Kruma said. A hint of contempt rode with her words as she studied him. Lecroix felt like a bug under the microscope of some dispassionate biology student.

"The Americans listen to everything. It is our best defense."

"Did they monitor your satellite communication in Idaho? How is it possible they tapped into a three-satellite link?"

"Given time, their NSA can work miracles electronically. Our best defense is to move fast and make no mistakes."

"Was poor Atta's body discovered and identified?"

"Probably," Lecroix said, not willing to bandy words. "Some

Americans are efficient at such things. I do not understand why, but they are angered more by the destruction of their trees than they are by the deaths of their people." Lecroix had kept close check on those who had been killed.

The forest ranger had been noted in passing, but one young girl killed by Red One had gathered the most "ink," as the Americans said. She was the niece of an Idaho senator, which had provoked some agitation in the U.S. Marshals' office. While Lecroix did not dismiss the effectiveness of the marshals, he knew his team had moved fast enough and effectively enough to stay ahead of them. Even in time-sensitive situations like kidnappings, it required a full day or more for them to bring the full force of their law service to bear.

The *Spirit of Brazzaville* would sail within the hour and put the gold beyond any U.S. agency.

"You are not concerned by your…mistakes."

"The mission went well. One loss, while regrettable, does not constitute a mistake. There," Lecroix said, pointing at the neutrally colored shipping container packed with five tons of gold from their numerous thefts. "That is success."

"You are right," N'Kruma said, smiling even more.

Lecroix tapped the cell phone in his hand and then turned it off as he walked to the edge of the dock. He watched the slow movement of the *Spirit of Brazzaville* as it nudged the dock with inexorable power. He had disposed of his satellite phone before leaving Idaho. Now it was time to make sure the U.S. did not trace this cell phone. He waited, then tossed the phone down so the massive ship completely crushed the device between hull and dock. The pieces tumbled into the oily water and vanished without a trace.

"Do you discard everything that way?" N'Kruma put a long-fingered hand on his shoulder. Lecroix blinked as he looked over his shoulder at her. The huge diamond rings adorning her hands were the product of death and destruction.

Blood diamonds, they were called, or conflict diamonds, mined by the poorest of the poor for the richest in the world. He had seen her lash out with a backhand that had stripped flesh from a man's face using one of those three-carat stones adorning her fingers. All the waiter had done was present her food from the wrong side. Lecroix had seen wounds in his day—that one required no fewer than a dozen stitches. For all her smiles and graceful, languid manner, she was as much a killer as he was. The only difference was preference in weapons. Lecroix used knives and bullets.

"I get rid of only the things that are of no further use to me," he said.

"See to the loading," she said, her dark eyes unreadable. N'Kruma smiled but there was no emotion there now. Nothing. Her warm hand vanished from his shoulder like smoke rising into a clear sky.

Lecroix knew better than to draw attention to the one special container. He stepped away and watched the dockhands work toward the sea cargo container holding the precious metal. Giant hooks came down from the crane, caught and lifted. The container swung about like a pendulum, causing the loading crew to curse in a half-dozen different languages. The gold had either shifted within the container or had been improperly stowed.

He stepped away farther to see what might be the problem. He reached for the SIG-Sauer in a shoulder holster.

"Ms. N'Kruma, go now."

She turned and looked from his hand on the pistol to the container. It swung more wildly now, but there was no danger of the skilled crew losing it or having to drop it. Dumping it onto the dock would be a time waster, but nothing too unusual. If they lost it into the water, retrieving it could take a day or more, since such accidents required the harbor master's supervision to make right. Most companies simply let their cargo remain on the bottom of the Bay. Shipping schedules being what they were, cargo in any one container meant less than delivering the entire cargo to its destination on time.

This was not a container that could be abandoned nor could Lecroix afford to have the harbor master and his nosy bureaucrats poking about a damaged steel container. Questions would be raised, especially when the RFID gave the contents as farm machinery bound for the Philippines.

"Can you take care of this situation?"

He glared at her. She smiled that mocking smile of hers. Then the smile faded when she realized how angry he was. A trained soldier with a pistol in his hand was not to be taunted. She nodded in his direction, turned and walked away as if nothing had happened.

Lecroix looked back at the container and saw the crew had checked the violent spinning and now was lifting it three stories to swing around and place it on the ship's deck. Lecroix raced to the gangplank and went up, running into the captain at the top.

"What is wrong?" The captain was Oriental and handpicked by Lecroix for this trip. He had once plied the South China Sea as a pirate. The sailor had proved useful, never asking about his cargo and always placating authorities in his ports of call. Oakland was particularly difficult, though, since bribing officials was frowned upon, unlike in more civilized parts of the world.

But there were ways to get the U.S. Customs and Border Protection inspectors to look the other way without greasing their palms. The captain knew them all and earned his exorbitant salary as a result.

"There was a man atop the last container," Lecroix said.

"Your container?"

Lecroix glared at the captain for asking such a stupid question. He cared nothing for the rest of the cargo already loaded onto the freighter. All the other containers might hold a million kilos of heroin for all he cared. The coincidence of a man choosing the one cargo container Lecroix was hired to protect, no matter what else the *Spirit of Brazzaville* might carry, was too great to ignore.

"I'll get some of the crew."

"No," Lecroix said, the feel of his pistol cold and heavy and familiar in his grip. "Continue working. I'll personally see to removing this problem."

The captain grinned wolfishly, obviously remembering his pirate days with some fondness.

"If you are sure. Good hunting."

Lecroix pushed past him and slid down the steel handrails to the main deck. He craned his neck as he followed the boxcar-sized container on its way to a secure berth on the deck. From his vantage beneath the container, he could not see the top, but he knew the man still clung there. It might have been some derelict who had the misfortune to go to sleep on the wrong container. American cities were filled with such vagrants.

Or atop containers holding tons of stolen gold.

Pistol held at his side, Lecroix made his way through the maze of equipment on deck. Three crewmen were all that were required to lower the gold to the ship. The crane operator should have spotted the man. Lecroix wondered if he might have been bought off. The Democratic Republic of the Congo owned this dock and staffed it with nationals who earned a hundred times what they might in Kinshasa, but they were paid in Congo francs. Though they might get into card games among themselves, no Oakland merchant would accept their worthless paper money, and finding a bank to exchange it was beyond their capacity.

Lecroix snorted. The worthless scrip used to pay the workers would be used as toilet paper if the crew realized the amount of gold bullion in that container. The crewmen might be ignorant, but they were not stupid. The look and feel of gold was instantly known to even the meanest street beggar.

The two cargo handlers on the deck, positioned at opposite corners of the container, guided it into place and fastened the locking mechanism that held it securely to the deck. Lecroix waited for them to move on before circling the container and finding the inset ladder leading to the top. Lecroix began climbing, SIG-Sauer in his right hand. He reached the top and peered over. Without hesitation, he brought up his pistol and fired.

The man crouching in the center of the container held a cell phone in one hand and a gun in the other. Lecroix realized he might have been taking pictures or doing any number of other things with the phone. The mercenary's first shot skittered along the metal surface like a stone skipping on water. The man immediately returned fire.

Lecroix got off a second shot and was rewarded with a tiny spray of blood. Then his own pistol's report was drowned out by the roar of a cannon firing. Dropping back down to get out of the line of fire, Lecroix cursed. He had winged the interloper but had not killed him. His first shot should have ended the thief's life.

Or was he a simple thief or a homeless person? The man carried a sidearm that counted as heavy artillery in some countries. From the roar, it was a Magnum or possibly a .50 caliber, carrying the impact of a large truck if one of its slugs struck. Such a weapon cost several thousand dollars—not the kind of weapon a derelict begging coins would have. This was no drifter who had the misfortune to get loaded aboard the *Spirit of Brazzaville*.

Lecroix grabbed a handhold near the ladder and swung free. He kicked hard and popped up over the edge. His target held the huge pistol in one hand and coolly pressed buttons on the cell phone with his free thumb. Two quick shots knocked the phone from his opponent's hand. If he was DEA or Homeland Security, he had just lost his link to any suppor he might request. But Lecroix wondered if there had been time for the man to order a raid or signal the U.S. Coast Guard to position a cutter in the harbor to block the *Spirit of Brazzaville*'s departure.

As far as he knew, except for the container he and the mysterious man now fought over, the rest of the freighter's cargo was legitimate. Orders had been given for this shipment to draw a clean bill and no customs queries.

Lecroix popped back up, ready to fire, but his target had disappeared. Scrambling, he got back to the ladder and onto the top of the container. He dropped to one knee and picked up the cell phone. A bullet had ripped through its guts, destroying it. He threw the useless device back down.

The tide was running soon, and the *Spirit of Brazzaville* had to get to sea. Lecroix stood and cautiously peered over one edge of the container. His target was nowhere to be seen. He stepped back, waved to the crane operator and got his attention.

In French he yelled, "Where did the man go? The one with the big gun?"

The crane operator frowned and shook his head. Lecroix almost took a few shots at the unobservant worker. He had seen nothing, not even the extra passenger atop the container when he had picked it up off the dock.

Lecroix flopped onto his belly and scooted forward. He sneaked a quick look, expecting to draw fire, but only the crew moved about. He agilely twisted, hung for a moment and then dropped the ten feet to the deck. A quick circuit of the container convinced him the seals and locks were intact.

He got the captain's attention and gestured to show that he had lost his man. Aboard a freighter this size, finding anyone who wanted to hide was almost impossible. If it had not been for the gold in the cargo container, Lecroix would have considered letting the *Spirit of Brazzaville* sail and then sinking it. The captain climbed up on the railing, adding to his five-foot-five height and quickly scanned the deck. He pointed toward a hatch at the side of the deck.

Lecroix worked like a broken field runner to reach the open hatchway leading below. He chanced a quick look before jerking his head back. The last thing he wanted was for his target to get off a shot from that powerful handgun. Lecroix would lose the top of his skull if a slug ripped through his face. He took in the entire scene and dropped through the hatch, landing lightly in a crouch. His own 9-mm pistol swung about restlessly as he hunted for a target.

The noise of cargo loading above drowned out any possible small sound his quarry might make. The vibration as the ship's engines were fired up made it unlikely the intruder would feel such movement. Lecroix advanced slowly, remaining in his crouch. He spun around a junction in the corridors and startled a crewman carrying a sheaf of papers. He turned instantly and went in the other direction.

As he hunted, Lecroix tried to decide which of the many intelligence agencies in the world might have sent an operative. MI-6 had shown interest, but not that much. The Chinese might have sent such an operative since their interest as both a supplier of raw materials and in the new markets in Africa was growing. Political influence could sway even the most democratic of nations.

Lecroix knew deep down in his gut none of them was responsible. This was an American operation. But which agency could it be? He would have laughed until he cried thinking of the CIA. The FBI was not good at infiltration and observation. The possibility that he faced a private organization sobered him. They could afford the best and followed none of the ridiculous "rules of engagement" that hobbled most U.S. intelligence agencies.

If it was a mercenary he hunted, it might be possible to recruit him. The Katanga Swords always needed a clever, dangerous agent. One with ties in the U.S. would prove useful. If he worked for another PMC, buying out his contract would be even easier than subverting a U.S. operative.

Lecroix smiled at the thought of almost five tons of stolen gold on the deck of the *Spirit of Brazzaville.* That much precious metal could buy any man's loyalty. After all, it had bought his.

A watertight door clanged shut ahead. Lecroix looked around. This part of the hold had already been loaded, and the crew had gone to work in other sections of the ship. But Lecroix was not gulled into thinking his quarry had actually passed through the metal hatchway.

Doors on either side were closed but not dogged down. Lecroix pressed his ear against one on the left. All he heard were the engines building power for the trip to the Philippines. A few odd sounds were caused by the crew finishing their loading above.

He dogged the hatch and turned to the one behind. This was little more than a storage locker. He pulled the metal hatch open a few inches, saw the shadow of his quarry inside and began firing. The slugs ricocheted within the small compartment, sounding like hail on a tin roof. Lecroix felt no satisfaction as he heard the thud of a heavy body collapse to the deck. He poked his pistol in, aimed and fired twice more. Both rounds found a target in the prone man's head.

He started into the compartment to search the body when he heard the ship's whistle screech three times. Cursing, Lecroix slammed the hatch, dogged it and then jammed it with a wrench from a tool kit left on the floor. He retraced his steps, climbed the ladder like a monkey and burst out on deck.

The freighter was in the process of casting off.

He shouted instructions to the captain, then ran for the

gangway just before it was pulled in. Feet on the dock, Lecroix turned and watched the *Spirit of Brazzaville* slide away slowly and aim its prow into San Francisco Bay. Sure that the gold was on its way, Jacques Lecroix walked with long, sure strides to where a car waited for him.

He was going to be a very rich, very powerful man soon.

The Executioner lay facedown atop Marshal Phillips's SUV as the lawman drove up to the main gate and pulled to a sudden halt. He had to grab hard at the luggage rails to keep from sliding off. The marshal was more accustomed to driving in the forests outside Boise than he was on dry pavement, or so it seemed. Bolan pressed himself flat, as if this would make him invisible. All he needed to do was stay out of sight of the guard behind the main gate. The short guard and towering SUV roof both helped, but Bolan kept looking toward the main building to see if another guard might be watching from a second-story window. So far so good.

"Howdy," Phillips called out. "I want to see whoever's in charge around here."

The guard came closer to the fence and peered through the chain link at the lawman.

"Go away. Nothing here for you."

"Well, son, you got that wrong. I'm a U.S. marshal, and have business with the main man. It is a man? These days, it's just as likely to be a female in charge."

"No women in charge," the guard said, grinning at the stupid American supposing for an instant such a thing was possible here. The smile faded. "Go away."

"You don't understand me. If your boss doesn't see me, he's going to see fifty other marshals come swooping down on the—" Phillips leaned out the window and made a big deal of reading the company logo "—Democratic Republic of the Congo's shipping docks. Now, I'm not saying it would royally piss me off to go to all that trouble, but I surely would not like it."

"Go away."

"You'll be the first one I look for when I get my search warrant. I'd hoped to avoid such unpleasantness, but the United States government's paying me whether I'm inside talking to your boss or calling down the wrath of God on your head." The marshal took his time putting the SUV into Reverse. Bolan saw the security cameras positioned inside the gate. They were aimed low, but he pressed himself even flatter and waited for the inevitable.

The guard touched an earpiece and nodded, although whoever spoke to him was some distance away.

"You want only to talk?"

"I can clear up this small matter in a short while. No need to call in the rest of my troops."

"Troops? You are a soldier?"

"Just my way of talking, though plenty of my men come armed with rifles and machine guns."

"You only."

"Let me in," Phillips said. The disgust in his voice communicated how close to losing his temper he was. Bolan doubted that was much of an act. Marshal Phillips was a man accustomed to getting his way.

The guard unlocked the gate and pulled it back on squeaking rollers to allow the SUV inside.

"Halt!"

Again Bolan was almost thrown off the roof.

"What is it, son? You got a bug up your ass?"

"I must check your vehicle."

"Do it and be quick."

Bolan's shallow breathing could not be heard over the purr

of the SUV's three-hundred-horsepower engine. The guard walked around the vehicle, poking about and tapping the tinted windows. He stood only about five-foot-six and could not easily see where Bolan lay on the roof. Finally came a gruff, "Go on."

Phillips floored the accelerator and roared through the gate, again giving Bolan a start. He waited for the guard to let out a cry of alarm, but the man was too busy getting the balky gate shut. As they had planned, Phillips drew up close to the main building, the passenger side only inches from the brick wall. As he got out, the marshal did all he could to draw attention to himself. He stood in the main door leading into the building, shouting for the manager to come into the lobby immediately.

That was all a diversion for Bolan to stand, get himself into position and jump to a second-floor window ledge. His strong fingers gripped the edge and then he pulled himself up. The window was open a few inches to catch some breeze off the Bay and yielded a way for the Executioner to get inside quickly. He tumbled into the office, hand resting on the Desert Eagle in its holster. He did not have to draw. The room was empty.

Wasting no time, Bolan went to the door and peered out into the upstairs corridor. Phillips continued ranting and raving to give Bolan time to get onto the docks and see to the container with the gold.

He made his way down the corridor, found a back stair and soon came out not fifty yards from the dock area with its bustle of dockworkers and clank of heavy equipment. The *Spirit of Brazzaville* bumped against the dock, moving with the powerful tide. Bolan felt the pressure of time. The freighter would sail soon.

He grabbed an empty crate stacked near the office building and hoisted it to his shoulder to use as camouflage until he got onto the dock. More than one dockhand bumped against him on the way. He grunted and cursed in French. No one paid him any attention. The men moving the containers onto the ship were too rushed to notice one extra set of eyes taking in everything.

Bolan stopped and looked around. He twitched, his hand starting for the pistol in its holster when he saw Lecroix talking to a tall, statuesque woman. From their posture, they were not exchanging sweet nothings. A man such as Lecroix would not easily tolerate a woman arguing with him, yet that's exactly what seemed to be happening. Bolan wished he could get closer to hear what they were saying. One thing came out of their exchange that proved invaluable to the Executioner. They both pointed repeatedly at one container sitting maybe thirty feet from him. He knew no other reason for them to single out this particular cargo unless it was the one he wanted.

The gold had been transferred from the railcars to a single cargo container, and this had to be the one.

It took all his willpower to keep walking. He could deal with Lecroix later when he figured out what the gold was to finance. Twisting, he dropped the empty crate and went to the securely sealed cargo container. Rather than break in, Bolan had a flash of inspiration.

He needed to track the gold to find the reason it was stolen. The container already carried an RFID chip, which should make it easier, if only he could figure out how to tap into the signal. Scrambling up the metal rungs welded onto the side of the container, he reached the top and looked around. This was riskier than riding the SUV roof into the compound because anyone on the deck of the *Spirit of Brazzaville* could see him. The crane operator picking up the containers and swinging them through the air to deposit in the ship's hold would be able to see him, too.

The steel cables supporting the container tightened, and suddenly Bolan found himself staggering along the top. The container began to tip precariously. He threw himself forward and grasped protrusions to keep from sliding off. His feet kicked out over the edge before he got a good grip and pulled himself forward. Hugging the container, he waited for the swinging to stop. A quick glance over his shoulder showed that the crane operator hadn't noticed the disturbance and paid no attention to Bolan. The heavy winch motor roared, and the container raced skyward again carrying the Executioner with it.

As he clung to the top, he knew his time to act was running out. Bolan pulled out his satellite phone and made the connection to Stony Man Farm.

"I need some tech work done fast," he said.

"What is it, Striker?" Kurtzman responded instantly.

Bolan heard Kurtzman bark to others around him in the Stony Man Farm Computer Room, getting their attention.

"I need to track the RFID in the cargo container with the gold. There's no way I can put a tracking device in it since it's sealed, and I don't have time to get inside," he answered.

"You want us to get a read on the RFID and do the tracking?"

"That's it," Bolan said. He heard more yelling. Kurtzman wanted an Able Team commando, Hermann "Gadgets" Schwarz, on the horn. It took only seconds for Schwarz, who was at The Farm between missions, to report in.

"What you need, Striker?"

"I've got a standard-issue satellite phone. Can you pick up the RFID signal and track it?"

"That's a passive device," Schwarz said, thinking out loud. "I'd have to ping it and see if I got a response. When I do, we can track it anywhere in the world. Hold your phone close to the center of the sea container's top. That's where they install the tracking chips on overseas cargo.

"I need you to send and receive some signals. Press the keys I tell you," Schwarz ordered.

Bolan came to a crouching position on the container. It no longer spun and now was being lowered to a spot on the deck. Two cargo handlers moved in and quickly disappeared under the edge of the metal walls. Neither had noticed him. For all he knew, men rode up and down on the tops of the containers all the time and he was doing nothing out of the ordinary. But if they caught sight of him holding his satellite phone close to the container and punching in sequences of numbers intended to activate the passive RFID device and force it to identify itself, all hell might break loose.

For the moment, he was free to work in peace.

"Another set of numbers. I'm close to getting the frequency. This is a top-of-the-line chip with some sort of password code needed to get a response. Probably controlled by firmware in a handheld programmable unit—which we don't have."

"Hurry it up, Gadgets. My time's getting shorter." Bolan heard clamps grating into place on the container. There were only a few more items to move off the dock to the deck before the ship would be ready to sail.

"Almost got it, just—"

Bolan didn't hear the rest of Schwarz's words. He swung around just in time to see a set of eyes peer over the edge of the container. He went for his pistol just as Lecroix fired.

The first bullet skittered along and missed but the second drove through the Executioner's calf like a hot ice pick through cheese, and then Lecroix ducked out of range. Bolan waited to return fire, but had no idea if he ought to look left or right, so he kept his sights where Lecroix had fired on him. The slight movement to the left caused a response both automatic and accurate. He sent a .50-caliber slug slamming into the container to release a shower of hot metal and bullet fragments everywhere. A quick glance above showed that the crane operator either had not heard the gunfire over the roar of his winch or didn't care.

Bolan started to fire again, but Lecroix got off his round first. The bullet caught its edge and sent the satellite phone spinning away from his hand. He dived after it. Whether Schwarz had succeeded in finding the right frequency and the password unlocking it mattered less than the link it provided him with Stony Man Farm. If he failed, they had to know right away.

But the Executioner would not fail. The satellite phone was just beyond his reach. A quick look down convinced him the device was trashed. The bullet had ripped apart its electronics. Without further thought of the loss, Bolan grabbed a stanchion on the edge of the container and flipped over. He hung for a moment, the cold steel of the container wall pressing into his chest, then dropped. He landed heavily, his injured leg giving out under him. The soldier rolled and came to his feet, hobbling off toward an open hatchway. Remaining on deck would only get him killed. The gunfire had attracted the attention of some of the crew.

One of them carried a slung AK-47. If one of the crew aboard the ship carried an assault rifle, there would be more—and Lecroix was behind him. The merc wasn't the sort to wound an enemy and let him go off to lick his wounds only to come back into the fray.

Bolan dived down the hatch and caught at the metal-runged ladder to lower himself to the passageway below. His leg hurt like hell, but it was bloodier than it was serious. His pant leg was drenched in blood, but worse than the wound was the trail he left. A quick look up the ladder convinced him Lecroix would poke his head around the corner any time now. He might wait and take another shot, but that only gave the mercenary time to muster the rest of the guards aboard the ship. Getting pinned down in this corridor was a one-way ticket to the boneyard.

He took a few seconds to whip off his belt and fasten it around the wound on his calf. The muscle throbbed now, but the pressure of the belt and cloth from his pants stopped the steady dripping of blood. Ignoring the pain was easy enough as he loped off. He had been more seriously injured and come through more times than he could remember. He ducked down a passageway to his left when he spotted two crewmen arguing ahead of him. They were on their way topside. If they spotted him and reported, Lecroix would be onto him like a flea on a hound dog.

Bolan came to a T in the corridor. The hatchway ahead led into the cargo hold. He heard men working there and knew he could never lose himself amid the mounds of containers. He went right, whipped open the hatch and crashed into a huge sailor coming out of the room. They went down in a heap, but Bolan's instincts were better. He drove his elbow into the side of the man's head. The sailor grunted and reached for what soon would be a bruise on his temple. Although lying on his back and having to deliver it awkwardly, Bolan used a spear-hand thrust to the sailor's Adam's apple. This ended both outcries and any fight the sailor might have had left in him.

Grunting, Bolan pushed the man off him and got to his feet. He looked into the compartment the man had left and saw it was a dead end. The commotion back down the passageway he had taken to get to this point warned him Lecroix was coming. Shootouts in metal-walled corridors never ended well.

Bolan opened the hatch to the left of the juncture and found only supplies stored there. He grabbed the unconscious sailor under the arms and dragged him into the compartment, then pulled the hatch shut behind. The cramped space didn't allow for much movement. Lecroix was no fool and would quickly eliminate the possible escape routes Bolan might have taken.

Heaving the sailor to his feet and holding him around the waist, Bolan readied the man to throw him through the hatchway the instant Lecroix opened it.

That was the plan, and it went wrong in a split second when Bolan's injured leg betrayed him by collapsing. The heavy sailor crushed back as Lecroix shoved the muzzle of his 9 mm into the compartment and squeezed off a half-dozen fast rounds. Bolan lowered his massive shield and saw the sailor had taken three bullets in the chest. He lost his grip on the man and fell back as Lecroix thrust his pistol in and fired twice more into the sailor's head to be sure he was dead. The last echo died down and the hatch slammed shut. Bolan regained his balance, lifted his pistol and pushed hard on the hatch, intending for it to fly open so he could squeeze off a round or two into Lecroix.

The hatch was jammed from the outside. Worse, he felt the deck shudder beneath his feet. The ship's engines were revving up. If he didn't get off the freighter fast, he would spend a long, long time dodging the armed crew—and Lecroix.

Bolan tapped on the bulkhead, listening to the sounds as if he had some special sonar in his head. The difference in pitch told him where the bar on the outside had been shoved into the locking wheel. A few light taps might work better than a heavier rap against the hatch. When this didn't work, he began a rhythmic beat and jiggled the locking wheel at the same time.

The sound of something metallic falling to the deck outside told him the hatch was clear. With a quick jerk, he spun the wheel and shoved open the hatch, his pistol leading the way as he stepped out of the storage locker. Lecroix was nowhere to be seen. Bolan chanced a quick look into the passageway and caught sight of a crewman scampering up the ladder to the deck.

The powerful engines moved the *Spirit of Brazzaville* abruptly enough for him to reach out to a bulkhead for support. He considered his options and none seemed too good at the moment. Whether Kurtzman could follow the stolen gold using the cargo container's RFID chip or simply tracked the ship as it made its way across the Pacific hardly mattered. That much gold was not going to be off-loaded anywhere short of a port with a heavy crane. If Lecroix tried rendezvousing with another freighter at sea, the recon satellites trained on the ship would alert everyone at Stony Man Farm.

Bolan had done what he could. It was time for him to split.

He glanced up the ladder and saw patches of clouds fluttering by in the brilliant blue sky. He took a breath, then scaled the ladder and popped out on deck, his pistol ready. The crew was nowhere to be seen.

Neither was Lecroix.

Bolan wanted the man so badly he could taste it, but the freighter was immense. If Lecroix had gone somewhere to hide, finding him could take more time than the ship's crossing to the Philippines.

Then he looked at the dock slowly diminishing in size as the freighter picked up speed. The distance was too great for him to be sure, but he thought he saw Lecroix get into a limo and speed away from the dock.

Lecroix had filled a body with bullets and thought his job was done. He had jammed the wrench into the locking mechanism to keep any nosy crew out. That meant most of the sailors aboard were not privy to whatever scheme Lecroix had cooked up. Maybe none was, other than the captain.

"You move, you die."

Bolan glanced over his shoulder and saw a crewman ten feet away with an AK-47 leveled at him. It was going to be a very long trip to the Orient.

"Got it," Hermann Schwarz said. He punched the Enter button on the keyboard and leaned back, looking smug.

"Striker," Kurtzman said, "we have a lock. We can trace the gold." He looked up at Schwarz. The electronics genius began working with increasing urgency and then sat back again. This time the smug look disappeared, replaced with one of worry. Kurtzman knew what this meant without being told.

"Why did we lose contact?"

"The best I can tell, the signal died suddenly," Schwarz said. "That could mean a lot of things."

"The satellite phone was destroyed," Schwarz said. "Striker wouldn't turn it off until he received confirmation that we had deciphered the RFID frequency."

"You want a pickup team sent? Buck can have one together in—"

"We don't know what happened. Striker can take care of himself." Kurtzman said what they all knew, but they also knew how dangerous it was going up against a man like Lecroix and the Katanga Swords.

"Continue to monitor the phone link to see if—when—it comes back online," Kurtzman said. "Call me if the situation changes. I need to get some sleep before I fall over."

"How long has it been since you got some shut-eye?" Schwarz asked.

"I don't remember." That was a lie. He knew to the minute.

It had been more than thirty-six hours of constant work keeping the intel flowing and updating men and women higher on the food chain. Kurtzman propelled his wheelchair to the staff lounge off the Computer Room. He heaved himself out of the chair and onto the bed, then lay back, hands under his head, and stared up at the ceiling. The air conditioner softly moved a cool current across his face, but he still sweated profusely and sleep refused to come.

"What have you stepped in this time, Striker?" he muttered. "What's gone wrong?"

JACQUES LECROIX HIT the dock just as the gangway drew away from the ship. He turned and looked to the bridge where the captain issued orders for his crew to maneuver the freighter. Once he was away from the docks, Lecroix would radio the captain with instructions to dispose of the body hidden in the storage locker. Identification would be impossible, but with the ship at sea, what did it matter who had crept aboard the *Spirit of Brazzaville* like some wharf rat?

"Are you ready to depart?" Coraline N'Kruma sat in the stretch limo, her long, seductively bare legs outside while she smoked a cigarette.

"At once. The ship must be met when it reaches port."

"Then let's not waste time getting to the airport," she said, flicking the ash from her slender French cigarette. He hesitated when she did not move to allow him in. A tiny smile curled her thin, ruby-glossed lips before she tossed the cigarette away and slipped fully into the limo.

Lecroix saw the company manager and a shorter man wearing a ludicrous hat walking toward him. Lugata spun and blocked the view for an instant. Lecroix swung into the limo and slammed the door. He had no desire to meet whoever Lugata brought with him to the dock.

"Drive!"

The chauffeur gunned the engine, and the long limo roared off. Lecroix craned his neck around to see the freighter now a hundred yards from the dock. He could relax for a short while until he retrieved the gold in Kinshasa.

"Would you like a smoke?" N'Kruma offered. "Before we arrive at the airfield?"

"No," Lecroix said.

"Perhaps something more? To celebrate a mission that has gone so well?"

She slipped around and down, but Lecroix thought of other things. Who had that been aboard the freighter? Not CIA. Not FBI. Who had it been and would their agency continue to meddle where they were not wanted? It was too much to hope that the death of their agent would deter them. The Americans might not be too bright, but they were persistent. It was good that he had slipped beyond their reach…for now.

"THERE'S NO NEED to shoot," the Executioner said. He held his hands out to his sides as he studied the crewman holding the AK-47 on him. Hoping for a man with a weapon he didn't know how to use became a moot point. At this range Bolan could get himself cut in two, even if the sailor had no idea what he was doing. Worse, he seemed both comfortable holding the rifle and capable of using it. His eyes were steady and showed no hint of reluctance to kill.

"You come," the crewman said. He might have been a competent marksman, but he had not dealt with men of Bolan's abilities. The instant he began the gesture with the rifle barrel in the direction he wanted his prisoner to go, Bolan sprang.

Hot lead ripped past and singed his arm, and then it was too late for the crewman. Bolan's strong left hand circled his throat and squeezed down hard. Inexperienced in hand-to-hand fighting, the sailor tried to pry loose the powerful grip choking the life from him when he should have kept firing and hoped to get a round or two in his attacker. Bolan pushed him to the deck and finished the job with a quick powerful jab to the temple.

The only problem in dispatching the man was the noise caused by the Kalashnikov's dull, distinctive report. Two more crewmen, similarly armed and also no strangers to handling their rifles, came on the run. The Executioner scooped up the fallen rifle and fired three short bursts that emptied the magazine. One round might have found a home in human flesh, but he doubted it. The *feel* wasn't right for that. He caught up the empty rifle and swung it over his head, letting it go when one of the crewmen stuck his head out from around a cargo container lashed to the deck. The stock dealt the man a glancing blow, but it was enough to get him to waste a few rounds of ammo.

Bolan knew that if he did not change the fight dynamic fast, this would turn into a cat-and-mouse game aboard the ship. He drew his Desert Eagle and fired methodically at the corners of the containers. One bullet ripped entirely through the steel shell and found the man hiding behind it. Bolan heard the grunt of pain and saw bright blood puddling on the deck. He swung around and got off a couple more rounds at the other crewman, who was trying in vain to aim his rifle.

The distant pounding of feet on the steel deck warned him his luck was drawing to a close. He tucked the heavy pistol into his shoulder holster, got to the rail and hesitated. The *Spirit of Brazzaville* was steaming away toward the Pacific Ocean at a good ten knots now. Hitting the water from this height would be like jumping out of a low-flying airplane, hitting concrete pavement and not having a parachute.

He jumped.

Bolan felt as if he had taken wing and floated. Cold air blowing across San Francisco Bay worked its way under him as if to turn him into a parasail. Then he hit the water feetfirst, and was instantly encased in an icy shroud. Down and down he plunged until his lungs threatened to burst. Powerful scissors kicks got him rocketing back toward the surface of the murky water. This should have been enough to get him to safety, but it wasn't. He had miscalculated the speed of the freighter and had landed near the churning prop wash.

The undertow sucked him back under. Mouth filled with foul water, he spit it out the best he could, squinted and saw the immense, slowly turning propellers inexorably pulling him to his death.

Rather than fight the props, Bolan swam toward the spinning blades. Testing the power, he found the spot where he could angle downward at the very edge of the vortex. Lungs at the bursting point, squinting against the turbulent water, he avoided the propeller blades and finally angled away from the ship. Still twenty feet underwater but free of the deadly pull, he simply relaxed and bobbed to the surface. He broke the choppy surface, sputtering and gasping for air. The freighter had continued on its course under the Golden Gate Bridge and out into the Pacific. Even if the captain had wanted he could not have stopped that prodigious bulk fast enough to deal with Bolan's escape.

The notion of survival trumped his relief at getting off the ship in one piece. The treacherously cold water sapped his strength each second he remained immersed, but he was still alive after being shot at more times than he could count. Bolan began a slow crawl stroke toward the Democratic Republic of the Congo dock. At first he did not think he would make it any time soon, then he spotted Marshal Phillips standing at the very edge, watching him. Resolve hardened within him. He would have made it eventually, but now his stroke sped up and he cut through the water like a knife.

Reaching a landing intended for smaller boats, he heaved himself onto it, sitting for a moment, gathering his strength and shaking the freezing water off his body. The sun was pale and distant behind clouds but warm in comparison to his swim. With every muscle aching, he got to his feet and climbed the steps to the dock.

"You call that a swim?" Phillips said without preamble. "Let me tell you about a swim I had once."

Bolan fought to keep his teeth from chattering. He was only a couple degrees away from hypothermia.

"It was in the South of France, along the Côte d'Azur at a nude beach. Warm, clear water, like floating back in the womb—and some of the prettiest naked women I've ever seen. Now *that* is the way to go swimming."

Bolan laughed in spite of himself.

"I'll try to remember that."

"The gold's on the freighter?"

Bolan nodded.

"No way in hell I'm likely to recover it for Lassiter Industries, is there?"

"Put in a request. I intend to get it back, along with Lecroix."

"If you stand around here much longer, you're not going to catch anything but a cold. He'll be entirely beyond your grasp."

Bolan looked involuntarily out to sea. The *Spirit of Brazzaville* was a tiny ship among many now.

"I'm not swimming back there to catch him."

"Lecroix got into a limo just as your ship sailed. I got it out of the dock's manager that he's headed for the airport to catch a flight overseas."

So it was Lecroix who Bolan had seen speeding away.

"Where? The Philippines?"

"That's the ship's next port, but my sources report that he and a couple others—working on getting IDs on them now—are on a flight over the pole to Seoul."

Bolan knew that wasn't Lecroix's eventual destination. He would change planes in the Korean capital, possibly getting on several more flights, before heading for Kinshasa—the capital city of the Democratic Republic of the Congo.

It was time for the Executioner to add to his frequent flyer miles.

The Executioner looked around N'Djili International Airport for any sign that the security forces took special notice of him. He had flown into Kinshasa from Tripoli, Libya, on fake papers proclaiming him on business for an import-export company. He had left Marshal Phillips at the Oakland airport, taking a small jet sent by Stony Man Farm to Nellis AFB for the quickest ride he had ever had. After being shoved into the backseat of an F-22 Raptor, he had gone airborne and ripped through day into night at more than 1.5 Mach to land at what had once been Wheelus AFB in Libya.

Bolan had been driven in the back of a quarter-ton pickup into Tripoli and had received his new ID and ticket on Hewa Bora Airways, the closest there was to a Congolese national airline. For what it was, Hewa Bora managed to get the Executioner to his destination without undue delay, even if the flight had been a bumpy one and had prevented him from getting any sleep.

Two security guards with slung machine guns eyed every white man leaving the customs area. Bolan had no reason to think they sought him specifically. For all Jacques Lecroix knew, he had killed some unknown agent aboard the *Spirit of Brazzaville* and ended the pursuit then and there. But the mercenary had not survived this long in a fiercely competitive, dangerous business without staying alert. Although the French mercenary might think he had killed one agent on his trail, there was nothing to think others would not be assigned. These security guards were likely paid to do more than maintain security. Bolan had to look at each and every one as a possible informant for Lecroix—and Joseph Chimola.

Still, Bolan realized he was being paranoid. Trying to leave the secured area of the Kinshasa airport in any way other than through customs would draw unwanted attention, no matter how good he was at evasion. Like most Third World countries, the Democratic Republic of the Congo relied heavily on its army to maintain order—or what the president and head of the army considered order. Outside agitators would be shot. So would any businessmen who appeared the least bit furtive.

Bolan walked briskly to the customs counter and dropped his fake passport on the counter. The agent looked up, bored, then took the document and flipped through it.

"Very good, sir. May your visit be profitable." The customs agent stamped the passport and returned it.

He tucked away the passport in an inner coat pocket and walked past the patrolling guards without so much as a sidelong glance in their direction. He knew they watched him closely, but would they give every tall white man this same scrutiny?

Without so much as a twitch in his direction, the guards let him depart the terminal building. He stepped into the hot equatorial sun and felt as if the humid air crushed him to the ground. It had been a while since he had been in such a lush, vibrant country. The hustle of cabs, trucks and commerce all around the airport showed that the Congolese people were not content to simply sit and wait for cooler time in the evening to conduct their business.

"Cab, please, sir. Take you to finest whorehouse in Kinshasa."

Bolan glanced at the earnest cabdriver, standing by a battered Jeep that might have seen service in WWII.

"Not interested in girls," Bolan said.

"I know places where you can find boys," the cabbie said,

as enthusiastically as before. Here was a man willing to supply anything, legal or not, that the Executioner might want.

"Take me to the air freight terminal," Bolan said. He swung into the passenger seat. The springs poked into his butt and the sagging suspension on the Jeep made him wonder if he would be tossed out if the driver took a turn too fast.

"Okay, can do that," the driver said, eyeing him sideways. "You sure you not want girls?"

"Not now," Bolan said. "Business first."

"Then monkey business," the driver said, relieved. "I can take you to finest whorehouse in all the Congo."

They threaded in and out of traffic, between more powerful cars and so close to massive vehicles that Bolan wanted to reach out and take the steering wheel himself to keep them from crashing headlong into the trucks ahead. He settled back and tried to enjoy the ride. The day was hot and the sun on his face soothed him, but he did not go to sleep in spite of his exhaustion. There would be time later.

He needed to contact Stony Man Farm and get an update on Lecroix and the gold as both made their way around the world from the opposite direction that Bolan had taken. Only quick reflexes kept him from being thrown through the windshield when the driver braked abruptly.

"Here we are. Then we go to whorehouse."

Bolan pulled out a wad of Congolese francs that had already become sweat-stained in his pocket. He peeled off twenty francs and handed them to the driver.

"Wait. I'll be back in a few minutes."

"Right, sir, you bet. I wait." The driver smiled a one-thousand-candlepower smile and settled back in the worn seat, adjusting earbuds and turning up his MP3 player so loud the music leaked out.

Bolan went into the air freight terminal and looked around for the ubiquitous security guards. He spotted two of them, both carrying assault rifles. A third patrolled the tarmac in the heat, either as punishment or because he was junior to the pair in the cooler freight office. It took Bolan more than twenty minutes and a considerable bribe to get the single case that had been shipped ahead of him from a location in Cairo, if he believed the customs stamps. It probably had been sent from Cairo but could have come as easily from London or Johannesburg.

"I help. Let me," the driver said, hurrying to take the case from Bolan, who shifted his weight slightly and blocked the grasping hands, one which still held the MP3 player.

"Take me to the whorehouse," Bolan said, knowing that was the only thing that would get the driver back behind the wheel and not asking questions about either his passenger or the heavy case.

Bolan dropped the case into the foot well in front of him and gripped the side of the Jeep as they roared off. A thoroughly modern highway led from the airport into the heart of Kinshasa, giving him plenty of time to study the traffic flow and the thick green jungle beyond. If he kept going in this direction, he would arrive soon at the seaport supplying the lifeblood for the entire country. Kinshasa's port of Le Beach Ngobila stretched more than five miles along the south side of the Congo River, with Brazzaville across the muddy, churning river.

"That is university," the cabbie said, mistaken in the belief that Bolan wanted a tour guide as well as driver.

"It looks prosperous," Bolan said. "Let me out here."

"What? No whorehouse there!"

"Why don't you go on to the whorehouse and enjoy yourself in my place," Bolan said, hopping from the Jeep and dragging out his case. He gave the driver five hundred Congolese francs, which soothed whatever lost revenue the man would have earned delivering a foreigner to the tender mercy of a cathouse madam.

Bolan looked around and deciphered the sign in French.

Where there were universities, there were hotels catering to visiting professors and delegates to conferences. It took him less than ten minutes to find a decent hotel and check in. Rather than create a fuss, he allowed the bellman to carry his case, although he watched his every move carefully. Choosing this hotel had been happenstance. No one, including the Executioner himself, had known he would come here. That added a margin of safety to his mission. Only when he had tipped the bellman and secured the door did he relax by dropping onto the bed. It was too soft and it sagged, but it felt as if he floated on a cloud.

His eyelids began to droop. When his eyes almost closed, he jerked upright and shook himself. There would be time for sleep later. With practiced ease, he opened the complicated locks on the case and found a satellite phone secured to the lid.

"Bear, what do you have for me?"

Aaron Kurtzman answered immediately, as if he had been waiting for Bolan's contact—as he had.

"Lecroix just landed in Mumbai. He has a ten-hour layover on a commercial flight. If all his other connections are made, he will land at N'Djili International within twenty-four hours, thirty-six at the latest. The *Spirit of Brazzaville* is scheduled to make port at a small Pacific island later today. It will be a couple weeks before it ports in Kinshasa."

"Then watch carefully for a transfer to air," Bolan said. "Things are moving fast, and I suspect they want the gold here as quickly as they can get it."

"Why put it aboard the *Spirit of Brazzaville?*"

"They must have done that just to get it out of the country. Having the dock under the control of the Democratic Republic of the Congo is the only reason I can see to ship it that way. No questions were asked as they would have been at an air freight terminal." He rested his hand on the case that had been delivered to him. Moving contraband in a small case was difficult but not as hard as trying to sneak tons of gold past customs agents.

"Who's traveling with Lecroix?"

"Your friend Phillips found that out. We actually had to call in some high-level favors to get him to stop his investigation after that. That man is a real bulldog when it comes to a case. The woman with Lecroix is Coraline N'Kruma, and he has two bodyguards. Or perhaps they are N'Kruma's guards. We can't tell yet."

"Who is she?"

"Well, when the State Department got wind of what happened in Idaho and Nevada and other places, they became very cooperative sharing intelligence from other branches of the government."

"She must be important, but I've never heard of her."

"N'Kruma is Joseph Chimola's mistress, but our spotty information says she might be more. Chimola is no one's fool, but N'Kruma might be the brains behind a revolt building in the eastern provinces of the Democratic Republic of the Congo."

"The gold is financing the rebellion?"

"The Secretary of State thinks so. Not coincidentally, so does the Secretary of Defense and a couple foreign policy advisers to the President. All have put considerable pressure on intelligence agencies, mostly to no avail. We think their lack of cooperation comes more from having to share than being pigheaded about territory."

"Chimola wants to set himself up as local warlord?"

"Oh, he's more than that already, Striker. He's governor of a province with considerable mineral wealth."

"And oil?"

"Buweh Province has vast amounts, and all undeveloped. Chimola is outwardly loyal to the present regime. The current president seized power twice as head of the army, but he is the Democratic Republic of the Congo's best hope of remaining even partially democratic. He has been elected in what most observers claim are fair elections."

"Fair for the region or really honest?"

"A former president monitoring the process has put his stamp of approval on the duly elected president. He might be a petty dictator, but he is a known commodity. Chimola is not."

"What's the downside of Chimola breaking off a province or two up along the Congo River? Whoever controls Kinshasa controls the river traffic."

"That's the problem. With the wealth of the eastern provinces in his pocket, Chimola can negotiate with powers able to bring in gunships to keep the Congo flowing free—for their chosen allies."

Bolan considered how what had looked at first like simple theft had turned into a major upheaval in the heart of Africa. With enough backing Chimola could again turn all of central Africa into a war zone as it had been in the days when Portugal still held Angola as a colony. The stakes were even larger now. Oil. Minerals. Political clout. China would back Chimola, since unrest in the region was in their national interest—and against that of the U.S.

"Chimola hired the Katanga Swords? Is that Lecroix's connection?"

"It seems to be. We have no idea what Lecroix hopes to gain other than a paycheck."

"He might see Chimola as weak if N'Kruma is the brains of the operation, but the brief time I saw the two of them together on the docks in Oakland, they didn't appear to get along too well. N'Kruma must be with Lecroix to oversee his operation."

"Lecroix might be trying to woo her away from support of Chimola," Kurtzman pointed out. "We have more questions than answers, Striker. Find them."

A faint sound drew Bolan's attention, and he cocked his

head to one side and listened. As Kurtzman continued with details he needed to know, including safehouses and drop points in Kinshasa, the soldier opened a compartment in the case where his Desert Eagle rested, silver and deadly. He took it out, jacked a round into the chamber and mumbled a bit as he rose from the bed to make it seem he was keeping up his end of the conversation and walked softly to the door. He put the phone down, silently took off the chain lock, then yanked open the door.

He was a second too late. The sound of thudding footsteps down the hall told him which direction the spy had gone. Swinging his pistol around he almost squeezed off a round, but the man ducked and turned down a branching corridor before Bolan could get a good shot. He closed the door behind him and headed for the stairwell near the elevator rather than trailing the spy. Taking the steps three at a time, he reached the ground floor in seconds and burst into the lobby.

Bolan lowered his pistol where it was not likely to be noticed and walked to the hotel's front door. The clerk glanced up and then went back to his work riffling through cards in a small metal file box. A dozen quick steps took the Executioner into the street. Looking around he noticed a familiar vehicle parked at the curb a few yards away. He quickly walked over to it, got inside and waited. Within a matter of seconds, the cabbie who had driven him from the airport burst from an alley, gasping for breath.

The driver jumped into his Jeep and started to race off when he stiffened at the feel of a large bore pistol crammed into his ribs.

"Looking for that whorehouse?" Bolan asked.

"You leave thing in my cab," the man said unconvincingly. His eyes were wide and sweat beaded his forehead. Bolan doubted all of it came from the exertion of racing down the back way. The man shook so hard his MP3 player's earbuds came loose and hung from around his neck.

"I'll leave a dead body in your cab," Bolan said, "unless you tell me who you work for."

"I drive cab. I know nothing else."

Bolan dug the barrel harder into the man's ribs. He didn't have to ask again. The man knew what he had to do if he wanted to stay alive.

The driver looked around frantically and licked his lips when he realized there was no escaping the Executioner. He started to speak, then clamped his mouth shut. His eyes went wide and then closed.

The gunshot that sounded a second later was curiously muffled. The driver sagged forward against the large steering wheel, causing the horn to honk raucously. Bolan pulled him back to silence the honking. He looked around for where the shot had come from but couldn't locate the sniper. Keeping his head low and his Desert Eagle handy, he quickly searched through the driver's pockets, discarding the paper money as he hunted for some ID. He found only the driver's cell phone, which he quickly pocketed, but nothing to tell why his cover had been blown so fast.

Bolan carefully climbed from the Jeep and, ducking into the shadows, made his way back to the hotel. He had more to report to Kurtzman, and nobody was going to like it.

10

The Executioner quickly put everything back into his case and left the hotel room. The driver had trailed him here before getting killed, which meant the cabbie's killer also knew where Bolan had come to roost. Going down the back stairs, he slipped onto the street. Blending in was difficult, since he was almost the only Caucasian to be seen in the throng of pedestrians. As he walked, regularly doubling back, sitting on benches and waiting to see if he recognized anyone obviously following him, doing all he could to lose himself, he thought hard on all that had happened since his arrival in Kinshasa.

The driver might have routinely reported anyone coming into the country who looked suspicious. Bolan realized having no luggage with him when he deplaned but picking up air freight had to ring alarm bells in any alert observer. He had foolishly thought he was going to be given a pass because Jacques Lecroix was still on his way to the Democratic Republic of the Congo and was not there to personally give instructions to the Katanga Swords. It might not have been any of Lecroix's men who spotted him, but the word had to be out now of a new player in the game of intrigue. Killing off a useful source of information like the cabbie would mean little to the men who hired him, but they would talk, either boasting of how they had capped someone who had gotten too close to his quarry or simply reporting the incident for money to others who might be more interested.

Like Joseph Chimola.

Twilight settled on a small park in the middle of the university campus, but the temperature did not plunge. Bolan wiped sweat off his face as he looked around. At no time during the day had he seen anyone following him, and he knew all the tricks. Two or three tails trading off the chore usually worked for all but the most cautious target. He had not seen the same man twice during his afternoon of wandering aimlessly along Kinshasa's crowded streets. Bolan was an unknown quantity, but a place like Kinshasa had to see dozens a day come through the airport that fit that description. With nine million people here and across the Congo River in the capital of the Congo Republic, such curiosity could run only so long before newer, more intriguing possibilities cropped up. Having two national capitals only two miles apart, separated by a huge river, had to spark incredible illicit activity.

The Executioner was simply small potatoes in a country already rife with conspiracy and intrigue.

He went to a bus stop, got aboard a double-decker bus and rode for more than an hour until he saw a threadbare hotel near the dock area where he could rent a room with few questions asked. Slipping the clerk an extra hundred franc note probably did nothing to insure his privacy, but it gave him a chance to estimate the man's reaction to the size of the bribe. Bolan had hit it about right. The clerk had not been shocked at a large bribe, nor had he been offended that his foreign customer had offered so little for warning that people—or police—might be looking for him.

The room was less well appointed than the other, but Bolan felt safer here. He adjusted the locks on the case and slipped it out of sight under the bed. Anyone searching the room would find it right away, but opening the case without the proper combination would destroy the contents. He stood in front of the mirror hung on the back of the door and adjusted his shoulder holster before settling his coat around it so that more than a casual glimpse was necessary to see that he was armed to the teeth. A sheathed knife strapped to his left forearm completed his armament for the night's excursion.

He returned to the lobby and looked around. Other than the clerk, no one likely to give a damn about him was in sight. Bolan walked out into the sultry Kinshasa night and went directly to Le Beach Ngobila. It was close to midnight when he finally located the docking area set aside for the *Spirit of Brazzaville.* A huge warehouse looked ready to accept all the cargo—but did that include the stolen gold?

Nose wrinkling from the stench of rotten garbage, Bolan worked his way around the warehouse and finally found an unlocked door leading inside. Lights near the dockside burned brightly, but the rest of the huge structure lay in a dim twilight that allowed him to move from shadow to shadow unseen. More than a dozen dockhands lounged about inside, some playing cards while others joked and jostled as they passed around a bottle of booze.

He slipped past the workers and carefully mounted metal stairs to the mezzanine, where offices stretched half the length of the building. Looking down from this aerial vantage point it was obvious that the shipping company operating the *Spirit of Brazzaville* moved immense amounts of freight. One cargo container would never be missed amid the thousands of tons that had to be shipped every month.

He dropped to his knees and tried the doorknob of what appeared to be the main office. Locked. Bolan worked a few minutes with his picks to open it. The difficulty he had opening the lock told him that something important was kept in this office. Duckwalking into the room, he closed the door behind him and went to banks of filing cabinets. He began systematically rifling the contents until a knee-high pile of manila folders beside him threatened to topple.

As he reached for another drawer, he froze. The sound of an approaching guard threatened to bring his search to a quick halt. The footfalls were slow, measured, nothing to indicate the man had spotted anything out of the ordinary. Bolan put one hand on the butt of his pistol while the other held a file folder detailing cargo manifests for the past week. If it came to that, a sudden unexpected flurry of paper in the air always created a diversion and gave enough time to fire the first shot.

The guard appeared in plain view through the glass office partition looking out on the warehouse floor. Bolan tensed when the guard stopped at the door. If he tried the knob and found it unlocked, someone would die—and it would not be the Executioner.

For several long, slow heartbeats, Bolan waited, and then the guard went on his way. What had prevented him from testing the lock was not obvious, but Bolan was not about to let a bit of luck deter him from his quest to find more about the *Spirit of Brazzaville* and Lecroix. And Joseph Chimola.

For a moment, he simply stared at the file cabinets, wondering if it could be that easy. He went to the C drawer and opened it. Chimola had a thick folder. He began spreading out the papers on the floor. His grasp of French was decent, and he knew enough to piece together the facts. Chimola was a major shareholder of the company operating the *Spirit of Brazzaville,* if not the sole shareholder. From the manifests tucked away in the folder, Chimola sent his ship to dozens of different ports around the world. This was strange because usually a captain learned one sea lane and the weather along it and seldom traveled anywhere else. From the invoices, Bolan could not figure out what Chimola was smuggling, but he made a quick note of the countries where the *Spirit of Brazzaville* had ported over the past few years. Kurtzman could check to see if gold thefts in those countries coincided with the departure of the freighter. Bolan guessed there would be plenty to link Chimola with thefts all over the world, and probably not only of gold—weapons, contraband of all kinds.

The sort of matériel needed to launch and support a rebellion undoubtedly had made its way to this very dock.

Getting all such cargo to Chimola had to be done by barge along the Congo River. Only poorly maintained roads and no trains ran from Kinshasa into the interior. Air freight might be possible, but why bother moving heavy equipment that might include tanks and APCs other than by river?

Another file showed a small fleet of barges that made routine trips deep into the heart of the Democratic Republic of the Congo. From the number, they could be moving anything. Bolan searched the records but nowhere did he find what the freight might be. Satisfied he had unearthed all he could, he returned the files to the cabinets and went to the door. He started to open it a crack to peer out but froze. Something was not right.

His mind raced, putting together everything he had seen and heard—and what he had not.

The guard had walked along the metal catwalk that served as a corridor for the offices but had not returned. Any number of explanations for this came to mind. The guard might have a cot in another office where he slept rather than patrolled. A phone might provide a way of him calling a girlfriend to while away the long, dreary hours of walking a post.

Or there might be a third explanation.

Bolan slid the Desert Eagle from its holster and jerked open the office door while standing to one side. If he had been in the doorway, he would have died from not one but two streams of machine-gun bullets. He paused a beat, two, three, then spun across the open space. He fired twice at the guard crouched at the head of the metal stairs. The first shot went whistling off into the warehouse. The other tore a hole in the gunman's head.

This sentry had been unexpected. Bolan spun back, avoiding a new cascade of lead. He thrust out his left hand and waved it wildly to draw fire. The next burst of machine-gun fire came up dry with a metallic click. He moved like a hurricane, bursting from the office and facing the guard who had stopped at the doorway earlier. The man struggled to slam a new magazine into his HK MP-5. Bolan gave him no time to chamber a new round. Three shots, all dead on target, dispatched this threat. Unfortunately the gunfire had alerted the workers below, and a quick look over the metal railing showed them all going for weapons. He had killed two guards and now had to fight it out with a dozen more.

He scooped up the dead man's machine gun and finished ramming home the loaded mag. As Bolan ran, he jacked a round into the chamber and gripped the handle. At the far end of the walkway he looked over his shoulder to see the vanguard of the men from below stepping over their fallen comrade on the stairs. Bolan emptied the machine gun in their direction. The leader yelped in surprise and lost his footing, either in the already spilled blood or out of sheer panic at having bullets fired in his direction. In the commotion, he collided with others behind him, giving Bolan a few more precious seconds to find a way out of the warehouse.

A quick look over the end of the walkway showed crates only a few yards below. The Executioner vaulted over the rail and landed heavily on a crate, one foot going through the thin wood top. Pulling himself free, he sat heavily so he could look up at the walkway. A head poked out hesitantly above the railing. Bolan fired. The report echoed through the warehouse like a clap of thunder. The big American missed his shot but heard frantic chattering as the guards tried to decide what to do. No one was going to peer down at him after his shot had blown a hole in the warehouse roof.

Bolan rolled to the side, came to the edge of the pile of crates and dropped hard to the concrete floor. He stayed in a crouch, listening, waiting. He holstered his pistol and drew his knife.

Two guards rushed around the corner, oblivious to their

danger. The Executioner moved fast. He punched one in the throat but immediately found himself grappling with the second guard. His fingers wrapped around the short machine-gun barrel. The man fired and the barrel got hot. Ignoring the pain, Bolan forced the barrel up and then back. The guard saw the danger and stopped firing rather than blow his own head off. That was all the opening Bolan needed. He hooked one foot behind the guard's ankle and leaned forward. The shouting guard went down hard, then died as Bolan's knife drove up under his lowest rib and into his heart.

Not one to waste good ordnance, Bolan grabbed the dead guard's machine gun and darted into the shadows. The large corrugated door leading onto the docks grated and clanked as it rose. For a moment Bolan thought he had a way out. Then he saw a dozen more guards rush in. They formed a line across the huge doorway, rifles and machine guns leveled. Escaping would require a bit more effort on his part, since shooting his way out was no longer likely. One or two or even a half-dozen guards posed only a temporary problem for a man with the Executioner's deadly skills. But facing this small army would be a challenge.

The guards advanced, then halted when someone on the dock barked a command in Lingala. Bolan didn't know what had been said, but the tone told him everything. He watched as a man in crisply starched camos strutted forward and stood with the guards between the speaker and Bolan. A considerable amount of shouting and pleading went on from the guards. All Bolan understood from the exchange was that the newcomer was a member of the Katanga Swords.

That name burned in his brain. The guards obviously deferred to the mercenary but reluctantly. It might have been his attitude or something else. Bolan didn't care. He drew his Desert Eagle, aimed and squeezed off a shot. The huge handgun bucked hard against his palm. Even before the recoil died and allowed the barrel to sink back down, Bolan knew he had struck his target.

The Katanga Swords merc lay sprawled on his back, arms outstretched as if he were trying to make snow angels on the concrete. For a heartbeat the guards simply stared at the dead man, then all hell broke loose. Whoever had led the guards before reasserted himself. Bolan realized he had made a tactical mistake in killing the mercenary. Taking direct command of men he had not trained with had introduced a wild card into the game. Now it was gone and the security guard's officer was feeling his oats.

Worse than that, the officer had to capture or kill Bolan now if he didn't want his own head handed to him by Lecroix or others in the Katanga Swords.

"There, go there," the officer barked in English. That made the Executioner pause. There was no reason to issue the commands in English unless the officer guessed the intruder was Anglo. From his hiding place Bolan saw the officer press his fingers to his ear. He wore an earplug and communicated with the guards up on the walkway.

One of them had to have gotten a good enough look at him to know he was white. The officer assumed English would be understood by any white man—and would lead him into a trap.

Bolan tried to see what lay behind him, the direction the officer tried to herd him. He didn't know the layout of the warehouse or how the cargo had been stacked. Trying to get back to the top of the piles of crates didn't look too appealing. The guards on the walkway became bolder when their hesitant peeks over the railing failed to draw fire. If he went aloft, he would be spotted in a flash.

Rather than retreat, the Executioner advanced, edging to another mountain of crates. A shadow on the floor preceded a guard. Bolan gauged his distance carefully, then swung hard, knife in his hand as the guard rounded the corner. A throaty gurgle carried only a few feet as blood from a severed throat drowned the man. Death throes twisted the knife from his hand, but Bolan followed the man to the floor. When he was certain the guard could not call out any more, he yanked the blade from his throat.

Still not wanting to retreat, Bolan backtracked the path taken by the guard from the dock.

He found himself in more trouble than he had anticipated. The officer had tried to trick him into going into what was undoubtedly a dead end where he could be finished off in a hail of bullets, but heading for the open door proved even more dangerous. The mercenary had not been alone. A truck unloaded a half-dozen armed men dressed similarly to the dead Katanga Swords soldier.

The officer in charge of the security guards spotted Bolan right away. Again, retreat would be a death sentence. Bolan swung around, spraying bullets from his captured machine gun. He winged two of the Katanga Swords and drove the rest to the ground where they began firing into the warehouse. The guards fired back, giving Bolan a split second to fall onto the pavement. He should have been caught in a cross fire, but instead he lay beneath it while the Katanga Swords fired at the guards and the guards fired back.

He crawled toward the door but found no easy escape. The Katanga Swords mercenaries were too good with their fire and had driven the security guards back—the ones they had not killed. Bolan got outside but could not get away without being spotted. The mercs turned their rifles on him.

The salvaged machine gun had come up empty, but his Desert Eagle roared repeatedly. One of the rounds missed a mercenary but hit the front tire of the truck behind him. The sudden explosion of air rushing out knocked the man from his feet. He went down yelling. For a brief instant the Katanga

Swords gunmen looked at the downed man and their truck with a newly flat tire.

Rather than take out one or two more of them, Bolan ducked into shadows and made his way down the front of the warehouse. By the time the mercenaries had recovered their wits, he had rounded the corner of the building. Now he did run. Hard.

He heard shouts behind and a few bullets whistled through the air, but they were firing blindly. Falling into an easy jog, he left behind the Le Beach Ngobila and finally melted into the bustle of the early evening traffic, doubling back to see if anyone pursued.

Bolan breathed easier at getting away so quickly. It had not been easy—too many were left dead—but he doubted the Katanga Swords would follow. He made his way through the lobby of the decrepit hotel and up to his room. After checking that his case was intact and had not been touched, he dropped flat on the bed and slept for the first time in days, content that he had definitively linked Joseph Chimola with the *Spirit of Brazzaville* and the stolen gold and had found new avenues to investigate for other thefts.

All that remained was to prevent the gold from being used to finance a rebellion in the interior of the Democratic Republic of the Congo.

Mumbai, India

"He's dead? Rostov is dead?" Jacques Lecroix tried not to show how concerned he was hearing this. Having to use a cell phone that might be tapped by any government in the world was absurd. It was worse receiving such shocking news from his informant about his men when he was helpless to do anything. Coraline N'Kruma watched him closely, and he knew he had already revealed too much with his words. From the contemptuous smile she gave him, he wondered if she already knew the details and had not bothered to tell him. For more than an hour, she had been speaking with someone on another phone. Lecroix needed to discover if it had been Joseph Chimola she communicated with, or someone else.

"Andre, not Pietr."

"Andre was a fool," Lecroix said. Pietr Rostov was his trusted right-hand man and indispensable for the fight to come. Rostov's experience fighting the Chechen rebels had already proved valuable. Tactics in the jungle were not significantly different from those in the urban settings. Only the terrain was different; humans were always the determining factor in any struggle.

"We do not know yet what happened. There was a disturbance at the docks that Andre investigated. He was cut down with a single shot."

"The warehouse guards," Lecroix muttered, thinking to

himself that Andre might have been "fragged" by the guards. He had always been arrogant, but his lack of diplomacy dealing with any of the men working the docks, including the guards, easily could have spelled his death. A casual insult to a man carrying an automatic weapon in a country like the Democratic Republic of the Congo was not the way to ensure a long life.

"They were fighting an intruder. Andre tried to take command and was shot. One bullet. Large caliber. That's all we know. An autopsy is in progress."

"How is Pietr dealing with his brother's death? They were close."

"He has vowed to kill everyone in the warehouse."

"Keep him from doing that." Lecroix recoiled slightly when his Kinshasa informant laughed harshly over the phone. "I order you to do so."

"I am a sniper, not an officer in the Katanga Swords. You contact him. You are the company commander, after all."

Lecroix fumed at such insubordination and the dilemma this posed for him. No one knew he had hired the sniper—the assassin's name changed with every assignment, but he was currently using the name Nogomo—but more than that, being away from the Katanga Swords allowed Rostov to direct them however he pleased. So what if it ran counter to what Lecroix wanted? Being almost a quarter of the world away robbed him of authority, and he had to admit that Pietr Rostov had a point. His brother's death had to be avenged.

"I'll talk directly with Rostov when I can," Lecroix said. "What more have you learned of the man Saseeno picked up at the airport?"

"Nothing. He disappeared like smoke. It was clever of Saseeno to contact me about his concerns. The man he spotted carried an American passport. Arriving without luggage and picking up a case at the air freight terminal makes me think he is another player."

"An assassin? Who does he work for?"

"I don't know yet. I lost an important informant when I killed Saseeno, but it was a necessary killing. The American had a pistol on him. While he knew little, Saseeno was not one to keep a secret if enough pressure was applied. The American could have offered him money."

Lecroix visualized Nogomo shrugging his slight shoulders. The man was nondescript in most ways. Thin, almost skeletal, no one would ever look at him and think "killer." That was part of Nogomo's appeal. He was an expert marksman, had information gathering tendrils throughout Kinshasa and nobody would give him a second glance. He was…ordinary. Most of all, Lecroix needed someone not in the Katanga Swords he could rely on should Joseph Chimola decide to switch allegiances. Chimola paid well and his schemes were revolutionary in every sense of the word, but he was more than a little crazy. Lecroix had seen his like before and knew how to hedge his bets.

If Chimola had Lecroix killed, Nogomo would receive a huge amount of money for avenging that death. It wasn't much of an insurance policy, since Chimola did not know of this sword hanging over his head should he double-cross Lecroix, but it gave some small feeling of revenge.

"Could this American be responsible for the deaths at dockside?"

Again he imagined Nogomo shrugging as he said, "Who knows? In this city, everyone is striving to gain power. He could be a pawn placed on the board by another warlord. I will watch for him, since I am the only one who had a clear look at his face, but he has probably disappeared into the city."

As Nogomo talked, Lecroix watched his companion. N'Kruma sprawled on her couch, sipping one of her hideous alcoholic creations provided freely in the VIP lounge.

Imbibing alcohol clouded the senses over time, and Lecroix had to remain alert every second of every day. He wished Nogomo was here. It might be worth a hundred thousand euros to permanently remove Coraline.

"Is there any unusual activity around Le Beach Ngobila other than the shootout at the warehouse?"

"Only the usual smuggling."

Lecroix glanced again at N'Kruma, one long leg indolently draped over the arm of the couch. She swung it back and forth as she sipped at her drink and studied him as if he were some insect under a microscope. Yes, he wished Nogomo was here, within range with his sniper rifle.

"Find out about the American. His presence worries me."

The connection went dead as Nogomo thumbed off his cell phone. Lecroix continued to hold his cell to his ear to give him time to think before dealing with N'Kruma. When he had settled his thoughts, he flipped shut the cover and tucked the cell phone into his pocket. One more use, possibly two, and then he would discard it to prevent tapping and tracing. Lecroix thought back to the man killed aboard the freighter. There might be some connection between him and the American who had so recently arrived in Kinshasa, but he had no way of knowing now.

He turned to N'Kruma.

"You look distraught. Is all well in Kinshasa?" she asked.

He quickly explained Andre's death and how Pietr might begin a pogrom to avenge the crime.

"You mercenaries have such a strange code of honor. Andre died because of his arrogance. Death was his punishment. The Katanga Swords are the stronger for his sudden demise."

"You call him arrogant? You should know," Lecroix said.

N'Kruma smiled wickedly, her vampire-like fangs visible.

"The gold will arrive just after our plane lands in Kinshasa," she said. The woman laughed at his surprise. "This wasn't what you meant? My arrogance in arranging for the gold to be airlifted off the freighter? I misunderstood you, then."

"You had no right to—" Lecroix bit off his anger. She toyed with him. She wanted him to be angry because it put him in his place and allowed her to flout her own superiority, even if it came from power reflected by the brilliantly shining Joseph Chimola.

"The time for revolt is closer by the day," she said. Finishing her drink, she placed the glass on the table in front of her with exaggerated precision. When she finally looked at him, fire burned in her eyes. "You take too long assembling the army and weapons needed. Joseph agreed that I should help matters proceed more efficiently."

"You've drawn attention to the gold. The Americans watch everything using their spy satellites. Revealing that it was on—"

"As if they did not know the gold rode on the deck of the *Spirit of Brazzaville*," she said dismissively. "He might have escaped."

"The intruder died," Lecroix said coldly. "I shot him."

"Show me the body riddled with bullet holes, and then I shall believe," N'Kruma said. "You are not conducting your part of the mission well, Jacques." She saw how he half rose and started toward her. Her smile infuriated him even more as she continued, "You won't harm me. You know what would happen if you do."

"You should have told me about airlifting the gold. Give me the details now, so I can try to cover the airplane's arrival."

"There is no need," N'Kruma said. "I have taken care of all that." She looked at him a moment, then smiled her vampiric smile again. "There is no need for us to quarrel, dear Jacques. We are on the same side."

"I know whose side I'm on. I have yet to figure out where your allegiance lies."

She laughed in delight at this, then signaled a linen-jacket-clad waiter for another drink.

Lecroix went to the floor-to-ceiling window looking out

onto the concourse of the Chatrapathi Shivaji International Airport to watch the endless parade of airplanes. Forty-five a minute, the lounge attendant had proudly told him when they arrived. Lecroix wanted to be on one of those planes heading for Kinshasa *now.* He had been stranded in the VIP lounge for almost six hours and had another four until the connecting flight departed. Having N'Kruma watch him as if she were a tiger and he was her next meal rankled. If he had thought for an instant that Chimola would not erupt in rage over losing her, Lecroix would have left her dead body in some airliner's cargo hold long ago. Let her see the world that way, rather than meddling in his carefully laid plans.

He stepped back a pace so he could pretend to watch the airport activity while he actually studied her reflection. She seemed perfectly at ease. More than once she had hinted at an alliance between them but had never gone so far as to suggest they oppose Chimola. Lecroix thought her flirtations were only bait for a trap set by Chimola. Should he so much as nibble at the cheese N'Kruma offered, he would be killed in any of a hundred disagreeable ways Chimola had learned during his years fighting rebels in the Congolese jungles.

Lecroix wanted power, but to get it he needed Chimola and his political connections in the Democratic Republic of the Congo. Once Chimola moved from the frontier provinces into Kinshasa and seized power, Lecroix would call in Nogomo's accurate rifle. Looting the banks in the ensuing upheaval would be easy, since Chimola would have consolidated them all into one as his first official act. No African ruler allowed money to leave the country during a coup.

A coup followed by an assassination, culminating in methodical looting of the country by the Katanga Swords. He only wished Chimola would be alive to realize how wrong he had been to hire a PMC of such highly trained—and ambitious—mercenaries.

"You dream," N'Kruma said. She sipped at yet another of

her vile cocktails but showed no intoxication. Her ability to consume had to have developed over long years of dinner parties and ever-so-polite conversation filled with witty rejoinders and flirtation. There was not much about the woman that Lecroix liked, but he respected her position and the power she gained from it.

Even if that position was on her back beneath Chimola.

"I plan," Lecroix said curtly. He pulled his cell phone from his pocket. This would be the final use. He needed to prowl the airport and find another cell phone, but that would not be difficult. For all its poverty, India had pockets of technology and sophistication matching anything in Europe. Any cell phone he bought here would be traced easily, but carrying it in Kinshasa might slow detection.

Before N'Kruma said anything more, he started pacing. Rather than rebound and retrace his steps, he left the lounge and found a spot near the lounge attendant where he could make his final call.

"Da?"

"Pietr, I just heard the sad news," Lecroix said. He listened to the Russian's bleak, dark rage and began channeling it into more productive areas. If N'Kruma had diverted the gold, Lecroix needed someone he trusted to guard it on arrival. Pietr Rostov might be a grieving brother, but he was the best of the Katanga Swords. Lecroix needed him desperately now.

After he thumbed off the power and tossed the phone into a janitor's dust bin, Lecroix felt a little better. Rostov would oversee the gold's shipment in-country. If only matters with N'Kruma could be as efficiently resolved. He bought a new cell phone from a vendor and then returned to the lounge to bandy words with the woman until their flight departed for Kinshasa.

Bolan awoke with a start. The hotel sounds had fallen into a drone of recognizable creaks and groans that lulled him to sleep. Suddenly something was different and it brought him to a sitting position, hand resting on his pistol. The muffled sounds of distant gunfire came from out in the street. Jumping from bed, he pressed his shoulder against the wall and peered out the window in time to see riot-gear-clad police moving in a line against demonstrators throwing rocks and bottles. When one glass bottle exploded, the Executioner knew the street demonstration could quickly turn into a riot. Any heated argument became deadly when one side lobbed Molotov cocktails at the other.

The police line advanced raggedly, betraying its lack of training. Some demonstrators used the gaps in the line to surge forward and pelt the police with rocks and vile gobs intended to anger. They succeeded. The police responded with water cannons and in less than five minutes had moved through the streets, pulling dazed, drenched men and women to their feet and passing them along to other officers who loaded them into trucks after binding their hands.

The entire demonstration could not have lasted longer than fifteen minutes, but Bolan had no idea what it was about. He'd just had his first real taste of everyday life in Kinshasa.

Placing his pistol on the bed, he opened the case and made contact with Stony Man Farm, giving a terse report of what had happened at the warehouse the night before.

"We picked up telephone activity from Lecroix," Kurtzman said, "both times directed to Kinshasa. It's a good bet he ditched the phone and has a new one. We're watching for it."

"I have a cell phone. Can you give me any information about who has been called on it?"

"Gadgets is on a mission, but I ought to be up to the challenge."

Bolan played every number in the phone book on the cabbie's cell phone into the link.

"I'll see what it takes to get addresses on those numbers. Most are likely to be other Kinshasa cell phones. Now," Kurtzman went on, "you stirred up a hornet's nest with the mission last night. The Katanga Swords merc you killed was Andre Rostov, a Russian national with considerable experience in putting down grassroots revolts."

"Does Chimola worry about someone trying to toss him out of his cozy province?"

"More likely, switching from putting down revolutionaries to being one isn't much of a change."

Bolan nodded. He'd had the same thought.

"What is going to boil the pot immediately is Rostov's brother, Pietr."

"Pietr Rostov? I've heard of him."

"Then you know how dangerous he is. You killed his brother, and he is not going to let such an insult slide. He's gonna come after you, Striker. If he finds you, he will not hesitate to kill you."

"What else is new?"

"Nothing," Kurtzman said. "Lecroix's flight arrives in five hours. An NRO satellite photographed the cargo container with the gold being removed from the *Spirit of Brazzaville* and put aboard an air freighter. Its destination is currently unknown, but what we do know is that it's not being flown directly to Kinshasa. That would be impossible to do without refueling, but there is some question about its route, even assuming it is going to refuel."

"Why rush things? He loaded it with the intent of shipping it by sea."

"That is unknown, unless whatever timetable Chimola has established needs to be accelerated. You should make contact immediately with the American Embassy and see what their information officer can tell you."

Bolan switched off. He knew the jargon. "Information officer" meant CIA. As reluctant as he was to approach any CIA operative, he had come to a dead end. The gold was airborne now, making his recon of the Le Beach Ngobila docks obsolete. All he had succeeded in doing was bringing attention to himself and angering Pietr Rostov. RFID tracking might still work, but he had provided the chip in the sea cargo container, not on the gold itself. If the container had been ditched, the gold could be flown into the country anywhere there was a landing strip long enough. Kinshasa, perhaps, but landing out in the province Chimola controlled was more likely.

Not wasting a moment now that he had all information available to Stony Man Farm, Bolan packed his case and left the hotel. He had paid for another night but would not return. If Rostov had found him, this would be a deathtrap. As he wandered about, hunting for a likely cab, he thought hard about the cabdriver who had been so expertly killed. If that was Rostov's handiwork, he already knew what Bolan looked like. Though it was possible the cabbie had been shot for reasons having nothing to do with him, Bolan knew this wasn't a coincidence.

The cabdriver had been killed because Bolan had been in a position to get information. How the driver had picked up on Bolan so easily at the airport was a matter that would be dealt with later.

The early morning street was crowded with commerce and the debris left by the demonstration. When he was sure he had a cabbie who had randomly passed by, the Executioner rode a few miles, got out, found another and then another to reach the front gate of the American Embassy. Going in the front door was risky, but he had no way of contacting the CIA operative inside to be escorted through a more secluded entry. He could wait for dark and try to sneak inside, but from what he could see of the grounds, that might be more trouble than it was worth—and could get him shot. The drive leading to the front zigzagged back and forth with concrete barriers strategically placed to stop a car bomber from driving full speed into the embassy lobby. Armed Marines stood in front of the gates with more just inside the tall metal gate if trouble boiled up. The building and grounds were more secure than most prisons, making Bolan wonder how the ambassador and staff felt working here. Did they consider themselves prisoners, never venturing out except to state affairs, or did they mingle freely with the people and then scurry back to their hidey-hole?

He walked to a guardhouse protecting the main gate and waited until the Marine inside looked up. Keen eyes gave him a once-over.

"How may we help, sir?"

"The name's Smythe. I'd like to see one of your embassy staff members."

"Who'd that be, Mr. Smythe?"

"Conrad Quinn." As soon as Quinn's name was given the Marine lance corporal stiffened and looked at him even more sharply. Bolan held out his passport. The guard snatched it from him and the matched picture with the man in front of him.

"Is he expecting you, sir?"

"I—"

"That'll be all, Corporal," came a baritone voice from somewhere behind the fence. "I'll sign him in."

"Yes, sir."

The corporal turned and passed Bolan's fake passport to the

man who had spoken. It took another minute before the double locks on the guardhouse gate opened and the Marine pulled open the door.

"Go right in, sir. Mr. Quinn will escort you."

"Thanks."

As Bolan passed the Marine, it felt as if he stepped into a different world. He had not seen the patrols just inside the fence, men with both dogs and electronic devices. These Marines paid him no heed as they concentrated on their rounds.

"Here's your visitor's badge," Conrad Quinn said. His own badge dangled from a blue lanyard around his neck. He was an inch shorter than Bolan but stockier, as if he spent too much time behind a desk. With a light step and sure movement, the Executioner wondered if Quinn had not been a field agent before accepting the information officer position here. The CIA kept a fair-sized staff in most embassies, and Kinshasa would not be an exception. From the tight security around the perimeter and the hints of motion sensors and infrared detectors along the pathway leading to the embassy, Bolan guessed that something had spooked the diplomats.

"Was it the street demonstration this morning?" he asked.

"How's that?" Quinn's bushy eyebrows rose a fraction of an inch. "Oh, the one down by Le Beach Ngobila? That was a labor dispute."

"Then your security's always this tight?"

"You're not from Langley," Quinn said. "You are very observant and seem to know our procedures. You could be from—no, never mind," he said, coming to a decision. "I don't have a need to know."

"But you're curious who I work for," Bolan said.

"We have been told by the State Department to render what assistance we could, which is unusual. Oh, Langley issued my orders, but there's no question that the Secretary of State initiated everything."

"That's something of a surprise to me," Bolan said. "I may not know as much as you."

"Come inside. Although the grounds are secure and swept for electronic bugs all the time, you'd be amazed what can be picked up using some of the newer laser gadgets. Or maybe you wouldn't," Quinn said, looking at the case Bolan carried.

"If you want me to surrender this, I will."

"There's no need, but everyone inside, all the way up to the ambassador, would feel better if we could, um, store it for you until you leave. There's no need for us to examine the contents, is there? No? Good."

They entered a side door guarded by another pair of armed and alert Marines. Bolan felt their eyes on him as he walked along the narrow corridor to an office door painted with Quinn's name and nothing else.

"We're not much for titles."

"Information officer is what I'd been told."

He stepped inside what appeared to be an ordinary office. File cabinets lined one wall and a large, government-issue gunmetal gray desk stood to one side. A lamp with a compact fluorescent bulb spotlighted a stack of documents on the desk.

"New decree from on high. Conserve energy. Go green," Quinn said without any inflection in his voice to let Bolan know if he approved or thought it was a waste of effort. He held out his hand. The Executioner handed him the case, which Quinn put in the top drawer of a file cabinet. He hesitated, looked over his shoulder and waited for something more from Bolan.

"This, too?" Bolan pulled back his jacket to show the Desert Eagle.

"Nice piece," Quinn said. "Keep it."

Although the CIA operative had kept a poker face, Bolan saw the play of subtle emotions that said any man carrying such hardware was likely to be death on wheels in a dozen other ways. And he was right.

"Come on into the sanctum sanctorum." He pressed his thumb against a small biosensor plate and stepped back as the door opened on silent hinges. The room beyond was so dim Bolan barely made out any shapes moving around until his eyes adjusted. Then he saw a half-dozen men and women busily working at computer consoles showing every inch of the Democratic Republic of the Congo.

"Constant monitoring," Quinn explained. "We keep watch on river traffic, anything taking off or landing—and anything in the streets of Kinshasa."

"What about Brazzaville across the river?" Bolan asked.

"Different country, different embassy. I'm in regular contact with the station there, though. You need information about the Congo Republic?"

"What can you tell me?" Bolan asked.

"For all their nearness, the countries are considerably different. The Democratic Republic of the Congo is just that, democratic. There are real struggles going on to overthrow its president, who is no angel, but he is as committed to maintaining a democracy as anyone this country's seen."

"So it's U.S. policy to keep him in power?"

"As long as the popular vote goes his way and he doesn't declare martial law, yes." Quinn turned wary. "Do you know something about a threat to the president?"

"Nothing specific," Bolan said. If Stony Man Farm wanted a station agent to know, someone would tell him. "The gold stolen in the U.S. is on its way. That's the only lead I have."

"All?"

"Maybe not all. What can you tell me 'bout the man who used this?" Bolan pulled out the cabbie's cell phone and gave it to Quinn. "The man was killed before he could tell me anything."

"How was he killed?"

"Professional job, sniper, large caliber, long range. I didn't hear the report for a few seconds, so the shooter was at least a mile away."

"Anything over point-blank is professional these days. One of the Katanga Swords?"

"Could be, but I don't think so. The cabbie didn't seem connected like that."

Quinn obviously wanted to know more, but Bolan was not going to reveal anything else at the moment. If Kurtzman or Quinn came up with additional leads off the cell phone, fine. Bolan wasn't counting on that to happen, though. Following the money—in this case, the gold—was his best bet. To keep the information flowing, turning over the phone to Quinn seemed like a decent show of good faith.

"The airfields in the interior are the most likely spots for the planeload of gold to land," Quinn said. "We can get you upriver. Your papers say import-export. That's rather clichéd, don't you think?"

Bolan said nothing.

"I'll have the documents section fix you up with a new set, with a different occupation that will allow you to nose about."

"Professor?"

At this Quinn laughed.

"We want *believable,*" he said. "I was thinking of something more in line with mining engineer or minerals specialist looking to exploit the wealth of the interior. It would explain why you were there and give reason to root around in odd corners of the countryside."

"What if nobody wants to be exploited?"

Quinn laughed again and finally said, "Everyone exploits someone in the Democratic Republic of the Congo. Pay enough and you get to exploit. Get paid enough and you want to be exploited." Quinn pursed his lips and looked as if he'd come to a decision. "How about the cover story of looking for new plants for some big pharma company? That gives a reason to be in the jungle without lots of digging equipment."

"I'm always looking for a new cure for cancer."

"Who knew?" Quinn shrugged. "It's probably somewhere in the jungle. All that's needed is somebody sharp enough to find it."

"How far upriver will I get before Chimola stops me?"

"Most of the way. He has river stations established here and here," Quinn said, pointing to a bottleneck in the Congo River on a computer display. "From there on, he is in complete control of the Buweh Province. Commerce, warships, everything."

"No trains," Bolan mused. "What about roads?"

"Bad. You could start now and not arrive anywhere you'd want to be within a month. In this country, the river is the only way to travel."

"I'll be in touch."

"It'll take a day or so for your documents to be created," Quinn said. "You might as well stay in the embassy. It's good talking to someone who's been in the U.S. recently. Most of the staff gets rotated home, but not me. Station chief is too time-consuming to lay down the reins for even a week or two."

"A slave to your job," Bolan said.

"You might say that."

"Thanks for the invitation, but I have other leads to follow inside Kinshasa. If the shipment's not coming in along the waterfront, that doesn't mean someone there can't give me valuable information."

"Don't poke around too much," Quinn said. "We have constant surveillance on all the shipping companies, including the national lines. Or perhaps, I ought to say *especially* on those. The Democratic Republic of the Congo's president is not a man to trust anyone else too much."

"Trust but verify."

"Words to live by," Quinn agreed.

Bolan collected his case and made arrangements to pick up his new identification documents at a drop point the next day. Already he was making plans for the trip up the Congo and for what he would find there. Joseph Chimola controlled the interior with an iron fist, having been appointed by the president as a gesture of conciliation toward a political opponent. What the president didn't know, or perhaps discounted, was blind ambition. Chimola was not out of the political picture but rather right back in it, and larger than life.

"What's the best way out?" he asked Quinn.

Without hesitation, the CIA operative said, "The way you came in. It'll be safe enough this time of day."

As the Executioner made his way back down the drive to the guardhouse and the silent, stolid Marines there, he slowed and looked back at the embassy. Kinshasa might be boiling with political intrigue, but something he had seen or heard in the CIA observation room had put him on edge.

The instant he stepped outside the gate, Bolan knew what it was. No fewer than three different factions watched the front gate of the embassy. By entering and leaving so openly he had become a target for political intrigue that went far beyond that offered by Chimola and his PMC Katanga Swords.

The spies at the gate had captured his image and probably forwarded it using their cell phones to higher-ups. Quinn had let him become a new pawn in a game of political intrigue that he neither wanted to play nor had the time to deal with.

13

Bolan knew he had walked out of the embassy into trouble, so he was already diving for cover when the first bullet sought his flesh. He rolled behind a burned-out car and came to his knees, reaching for his pistol. He scanned the area where the shots had to have come from, but saw nothing. A quick glance in the direction of the embassy showed the Marines were alert but not willing to come to his aid. He guessed that they had standing orders not to be decoyed from their posts.

The Executioner was on his own. As usual.

He moved from the dubious safety of the burned-out car and found a more secure spot at the corner of a building on a major street leading away from the embassy. He considered calling Quinn, but by the look of the monitoring station that Bolan had seen behind the man's office, the CIA agent likely already knew every detail of the streetfight.

Was there some reason he wanted Bolan to get filled with lead?

Picking up his case, Bolan walked down the street, keeping the brick buildings at his right side for protection. The broad street filled with trucks and cars afforded no safety for him. Snipers could pick him off from any of a dozen places. Ahead and behind, though, were the most likely places for a killer to lurk on foot—anyone in the thick of the crowd might be waiting to pump a few point-blank rounds into his belly or back.

As he walked, the big American sifted through all he had

learned that morning from the CIA station master. Kinshasa was torn into a dozen different warring factions, with the democratically elected president doing what he could to hold together uneasy alliances. All Joseph Chimola had to do was gain control of the interior's mineral wealth and there would be a new leader for the Democratic Republic of the Congo—and it wasn't likely to be the current U.S.-supported one.

Bolan realized his visit to the embassy might have been ill conceived. So many power games were playing out that he wondered if anyone bothered to keep them all straight. As hard as it was to believe, he knew that Quinn—and the CIA—might be playing a game different from the one sending the Executioner into the country. The State Department, and presumably the President, wanted the Democratic Republic of the Congo to grow from the turmoil that beset it now. If the CIA had chosen another course, two arms of the U.S. might be wrestling each other.

Nothing in Quinn's briefing had led Bolan to believe the CIA had any interest in supporting Joseph Chimola's bid for power. But even if it had, the Executioner had a mission and that mission was to remove Chimola as a threat.

He backed into a boarded-up doorway of a burned-out jewelry store and waited to see if anyone followed him. Two men looking out of place in business suits and ties walked a few feet apart on the sidewalk trying to appear unconnected, but they were together. Occasional glimpses of one to the other coordinated their search. Bolan touched the butt of his Desert Eagle, but he did not pull it out. On a crowded street like this, any gunplay could result in the deaths of more innocents than villains.

When the pair came within ten yards of where he pressed into the doorway, they turned to each other and rattled off a conversation in Lingala too fast for Bolan to decipher. The few words he knew of the local lingua franca were limited to swear words and the more important verbs. He wished they had conducted their talk in French. He knew more of that language.

The language he knew best of all was action.

Using his elbow, he broke through a board behind him and slid his case to safety. When he was sure it was hidden from casual observation from the street, he stepped out and walked directly to the closer man who had been tailing him. The man's partner spotted Bolan before his intended target did.

A hard jab to the man's midriff doubled him over. His Beretta 92-S clanked on the sidewalk. With practiced moves, Bolan kicked the pistol toward the wall, swung behind the man, got him in a chokehold and applied enough pressure to make him go limp. A few more seconds of pressure would kill the man. Bolan swung him around to use as a shield when his partner lifted a small-caliber pistol and aimed it in Bolan's direction.

"No matter what happens, he's dead," Bolan said. "You, too, unless you're a better shot than it appears."

The man's hand shook so hard any bullet he fired would miss by a country mile.

"We want to talk."

Bolan saw how the pedestrians all around them on the sidewalk backed away. It would be only a few minutes before a police officer came to see what the dispute was about. Or maybe, in this part of town where commerce was conducted and embassies lined the streets, soldiers would be sent. In either case, Bolan wanted to avoid the authorities. Quinn might get him out of jail, but it was better to avoid that entirely if he wanted to keep a low profile. Or at least one lower than being carted off to prison by a dozen policemen because he had killed two well-dressed men who seemed intent on killing him.

A battered panel van screeched around the corner and cut across two lanes of traffic. Bolan saw it coming and ducked, holding his hostage in front of him as a hail of bullets blasted away the brick behind him and vital organs inside the man he restrained in a chokehold. The other man with the shaky gun hand caught a half-dozen rounds in the back and died before he hit the sidewalk.

Inside the open van door crouched two men, both wearing a black balaclava and spraying machine-gun bullets wildly.

Bolan sagged, taking his now-dead shield with him. He grabbed the Beretta off the concrete and began firing into the van. One man doubled over and fell into the street. When the magazine on his captured weapon came up empty, the Executioner dropped the pistol and drew his own.

The driver floored the accelerator, but Bolan took careful aim and fired. The driver died at the wheel, causing the van to jump the curb and smash into a storefront amid a shower of glass and broken brick. The crash, if the gunfight hadn't already produced loud cries of indignation and fear, coupled with alarms ringing up and down the street. A quick glance around told the Executioner it was time to move on. More than a dozen people held cell phones to their ears and gestured frantically with their free hands. It didn't take much to guess that they were all talking to the authorities.

Sirens in the distance approached rapidly. Bolan patted down the man still in his arms, but he carried no wallet or other ID. Dropping him and holstering his pistol, Bolan walked back down the street to where he had left his case with all the equipment sent by Stony Man Farm. Before he could wrestle with a couple boards and reach the case, a police car skidded to a halt at the curb behind him. Bolan turned smoothly and walked away while the policemen's attention was focused on the bodies on the street and the damaged clothing shop. He quickly turned the corner and sprinted to the next block, where he slowed to a more sedate pace. Even in Kinshasa, a running man attracted unwanted attention.

Bolan got his bearings, since he had to return to pick up his case, but that could wait until the dust had settled. He pulled his coat around and smoothed wrinkles from it to hide the bulge made by his Desert Eagle. A quick check of his watch showed that he had walked from the front gate of the American Embassy only a half hour earlier. It felt as if he had been on the run for days.

Strolling down the crowded street, Bolan stopped often to window-shop—and check the reflection for anyone paying attention to him.

When he spotted a dilapidated Saab pacing him, he crossed the street and doubled back. The car was having difficulty making a U-turn in the heavy traffic without causing a wreck. Bolan ducked into a large department store, counted to one hundred, then left the way he had entered. The battered car was just turning the far corner, its driver assuming their target would seek another door out of the store.

The Executioner had barely taken a dozen steps when he was aware of two men flanking him. He started to his left when he saw the flash of gunmetal, only to freeze when another pistol muzzle was jammed into his back.

"Come with us or die right here."

Bolan tensed to take out the man threatening him, but as he turned he stopped. The old Saab was parked at the curb. A man with an M-16 sat in the passenger seat, aiming directly at him. Unlike the gunman that he'd encountered earlier that morning, this shooter had the steady nerves and keen eye of an expert marksman.

If they had wanted him dead, another drive-by would have been easily completed. He yanked free as one man went to take his pistol. Rifle or not, he was going to put up a fight.

"Let him keep it. He is not going to use it. Not now."

This struck Bolan as a curious thing to say. He took a better look at his captors. The two men on either side of him were darker skinned than the rifleman, with broader features and the trace of a French accent. That they had spoken English told him they wanted him to know what was going on—or at least not put up a fuss for a few minutes. Letting him keep his pistol under any circumstances was foolish unless all they really wanted to do was talk.

He slid into the backseat, sandwiched by the two. The man in the passenger seat turned and stared at him. All his captors were shabbily dressed, but both the driver and the rifleman had manicured nails and the look of easy living. Not so the pair keeping him pinned between them in the backseat.

"You are CIA." This was not a question but a flat statement. The man with the M-16 appeared to be the leader.

"It wouldn't do me any good denying it," Bolan said.

"Blindfold him." The instant Bolan tensed, the man said, "We let you keep your formidable weapon. If we wanted you dead, it would have happened the minute you stepped out of the embassy."

"Not so smart of me showing myself like that, was it?"

"How else would you have found us?"

"What makes you think I wanted to find you?" Bolan asked.

"There is no other way for you to get into the interior quickly."

"You run a ferry service?"

"You are smart man. We saw how you handled Chimola's thugs and the others. Who were they?"

"Which were Chimola's men?"

"The van! They were the ones in the van!"

"I don't know who the men in suits were."

This sparked a lengthy four-way argument among his captors.

"The blindfold. Now."

Bolan sank back in the seat so a black cloth bag could be slipped over his head. He rocked his head back even more to let the hot equatorial sun shine down on his masked face. As the car drove up one street and then down another in the opposite direction, Bolan kept track of where he was by the way the heat from the sun moved. Added to his estimate of speed and distance, he had a good idea where they took him. He had explored the western end of Le Beach Ngobila, and now he was being taken somewhere at the eastern end. He heard the movement of ships on the Congo River, complete with whistles and the sounds of cargo flowing into the country.

"Out. Here." He was shoved forward as the bag was yanked off his head. They stood in a warehouse much smaller than the one where he had expected the stolen gold to be unloaded. The other warehouse, besides being larger and filled with cargo crates, had been better kept. He saw sunlight lancing through the metal walls of this warehouse, giving him still more information about where it was located. If he went out the door they had entered by, he would have less than a hundred yards' march to reach the docks on the Congo River.

He faced the men. They moved easily and handled their weapons with familiarity.

"You are CIA and want to overthrow Joseph Chimola."

"Rebels?" His question took them aback. The leader recovered first.

"We ask questions. You answer or we kill you."

"Are you up to it? At the other end of the docks they thought they were. In Chimola's warehouse last night. Bodies all over the place."

"You?" The man's eyes went wide. "You alone killed so many of them?"

"Including Andre Rostov," Bolan said precisely, waiting for the effect.

"He was the brother of Pietr Rostov, the Katanga Swords' commander." More than a hint of admiration tinged the man's words. For the rest of it, Bolan detected a longing.

"You wanted to kill him?"

"Both Rostovs!" The leader realized he was revealing more than he was getting in the way of information. "They killed my family, my village."

"You look like a city-bred rebel to me," Bolan said.

"Every one of us they kill is a death in our family," the driver chimed in.

"Solidarity," Bolan said, nodding. "I killed Andre Rostov. I'll kill Pietr Rostov if he gets in my way, but Jacques Lecroix is the leader of the Katanga Swords. I want him."

The four chattered among themselves, all speaking at the same time. Finally, the leader nodded curtly.

"You are, what do they say? The right stuff."

"You'll take me upriver if I promise to kill Rostov, Lecroix and Chimola?"

"No. We take you up the river to stop the killing. If it means their deaths, fine." He smiled wickedly, showing dazzling white teeth except for two gold ones. He touched them and said, "A Katanga Swords' interrogator had begun pulling out my teeth with pliers. You do not have to kill them. We will…with pleasure. But they are powerful, well armed and trained. Stop all of them from killing more of our people."

"They learn the country by stalking our people," the driver cut in.

"They practice on us as if we were nothing more than wild game for their amusement. We are organized to fight, but they use electronic equipment and the finest of weapons."

"Airships!"

Bolan said nothing as the story spilled out, each of the men taking a turn to relate some atrocity done in Chimola's name by Rostov or another of the Katanga Swords. A picture began to form of the interior provinces deep inside the Democratic Republic of the Congo. Jacques Lecroix was Chimola's right-hand man, his enforcer and the one who issued orders to the Katanga Swords. This insulated Chimola from getting his hands bloody personally, but no order was given that did not bubble up from the filthy cauldron of the provincial governor's mind. Chimola used his position to crush any rebellion from the towns surrounding his sprawling villa in what he had made the capital of the Buweh Province. The entire area had become a huge armed camp. This much Bolan had learned from Quinn, but the CIA agent had not detailed armed resistance or how to contact the guerrillas.

"You will lead us. You know how to fight. We are farmers," pleaded one of the two men who had been in the back of the car guarding Bolan.

He suspected there was more to that entreaty than wanting a trained leader. They wanted U.S. aid and thought the CIA could provide it. Considering how little they had to fight with, that any of them had survived this long seemed quite an accomplishment to the Executioner.

"I'll need to know more," he said. "Numbers, arms, how well trained you are."

"You will go upriver, then we show you all this. It is dangerous in Kinshasa."

"Who were the men in the suits that Chimola's gunmen killed?"

The driver shrugged, then said, "There are many factions. You are American. Americans are rich."

It was becoming increasingly clearer to Bolan that Quinn had set up the meeting in the embassy to flush out all the malcontents and revolutionaries in Kinshasa. He had been used as a stalking horse for the CIA and didn't appreciate it. By going along with the rebels, he could get passage up the Congo without using the CIA operative's resources.

"How do you intend to get me past the checkpoints Chimola has along the river? He controls everything going in and out of the province along the river."

"We know paths through the jungle," the leader assured him. "We land before reaching the security fort, then walk into Buweh."

Bolan had started to ask more about the revolt against

Chimola and who led it when screeching tires caused him to go for the huge pistol holstered under his left arm. He dragged out the Desert Eagle and fired as the door opened. The slug caught a man dressed in the same camo pattern that Andre Rostov had worn.

"Katanga Swords!"

This was the last thing the driver uttered before a shotgun blast cut him in two. A dozen PMC mercs crowded into the warehouse, all firing as they entered. Bolan got off one more shot that missed and then was forced to take cover from the hail of bullets coming his way. He skidded along the floor and found himself behind the same crate as the rifleman from the car.

"How do we get out?" Bolan asked.

"We can't. We are trapped," the leader of the rebels said grimly. Then he stood, leveled his M-16 and began firing methodically at the Katanga Swords advancing on their position.

Stony Man Farm, Virginia

"What's the status?" Barbara Price asked.

"I lost contact with Striker immediately after he left the embassy."

"That was an hour ago," the mission controller said.

"From the scrambled radio traffic we picked up, the CIA station chief set him up for an ambush."

"What?"

"I can't get hard evidence on it—yet. Quinn knew there were several opposing factions waiting outside the embassy. They keep it under constant surveillance."

"The CIA uses this observation to track the groups," Price said, nodding. "Smart, but not when they jeopardize our mission."

"And our guy," Kurtzman said. "Striker started off on foot after an exchange of gunfire immediately outside the embassy gates. From what I can tell, there were several bodies left not a quarter mile off along a commercial district."

"That's our Striker," she said with grim satisfaction. "What then?"

"I lost him. The case we sent with all the electronics and comm gear has remained stationary. However, there's no reason to believe it wasn't stashed to keep it from falling into the wrong hands."

"In Kinshasa, which are the right hands? Even those on our

side, supposedly, might not be the best to retrieve the case. Can you send a destruct signal to it?"

Kurtzman shook his head. It felt as if it would explode from the headache that had built up. He had slept a little, but not enough. Though if it required him to go another forty hours without sleep to see Bolan through the mission successfully, he would do it.

"The plane," Kurtzman said, "with Lecroix and Coraline N'Kruma will land within a few hours. Although it is a commercial airliner, I believe the plane is flying directly to the Buweh Province airstrip. There has been considerable radio contact to this effect. The pilot is rejecting the notion, but controllers on the ground are taking Chimola's side. They have probably been paid off."

"Is the airport large enough to land a jumbo jet? The last reports I saw said it was hardly more than a cleared strip of jungle."

"Chimola has been busy," Kurtzman said. "The first thing he did, after getting a boatload of stolen gold late last year, was improve the airport. While it might enhance commerce in the region, its purpose is more likely to land heavy artillery and perhaps even tanks purchased from the Russians."

"He hasn't enough money, even with the tons of gold already stolen, to buy too much. Or does he?"

"He's avoided the blood diamond trade, if that's what you mean. The tanks we believe he has purchased are outdated T-72 Soviet models with 125-mm guns that have been rusting in a field outside Kiev. The Ukrainians don't want them since they might be slightly radioactive, which is why the Russians abandoned them right after Chernobyl." Kurtzman took a drink of the cold coffee in a cup beside his keyboard and made a face. The coffee had not improved with age. "Maybe the radiation from Chernobyl preserved them."

"But they'll be good enough for Chimola's needs. He won't

be up against anything more than RPGs," Price agreed. "A few outmoded tanks would let Chimola run roughshod over all the provinces. The president's army has nothing to match even a battered Soviet-built tank," Price stated.

"That's his most likely plan. With the Katanga Swords as his personal army, he can cut Kinshasa off from both agricultural and mineral resources."

"No minerals means no trade. There are about eight million mouths to feed in Kinshasa alone. I doubt their roughly two million friends across the river in Brazzaville will be any help, since the Congo Republic is bankrupt."

"Striker has to stop Chimola soon," Kurtzman said.

"See to it, Bear." With that Price walked off to brief Hal Brognola. Kurtzman turned back to monitoring intel from the spy satellites trained on Buweh Province and Chimola's training camps.

"WE WILL BE ON THE GROUND within three hours," Jacques Lecroix said. "Muster the Katanga Swords. I want to speak to them as soon as possible." He clicked off his phone and leaned back in the seat. It felt lumpy under him, irritating and completely unacceptable. He would prefer to be in the jungle training with his men rather than letting Pietr Rostov do the chore. Ever since his brother had been killed, Rostov sounded increasingly unstable. Lecroix wanted to be on hand to keep the morose Russian under control.

"Trouble?" Coraline N'Kruma looked at him—through him.

"What is the status of the cargo plane?" Lecroix looked across the aisle to the other passengers in first class. Both of them slept or appeared to. He wished he had his own jet so he wouldn't have to worry about being overheard on commercial flights. He would. Soon. Let Chimola seize control of all the Democratic Republic of the Congo; Kinshasa and the country would fall quickly. From there it was only a matter of time until he wrested political control from the would-be dictator. The Katanga Swords were loyal to him, not to a two-bit dictator from the back country of a Third World nation.

"It will arrive soon after we do," N'Kruma said.

He worried about the woman more than he did Rostov or Chimola or the hurdles they faced in seizing control of the Democratic Republic of the Congo. She had Chimola wrapped around her little finger. The huge diamond ring she wore was only part of it. Chimola had insisted that the diamond be legally purchased from a licensed dealer rather than finding a conflict diamond for a tenth of the price. For a man who remorselessly ordered the deaths of hundreds of his countrymen on a daily basis, Chimola had curious sensitivities.

"We need to pay the Russian arms dealer immediately. The gold should be deposited in an offshore bank."

"Indeed," she said, sipping her drink. The way her eyes bored into him caused him to sit a little straighter. She had ordered the gold removed from the *Spirit of Brazzaville* and had not told him. The stolen gold—gold gained through his planning and the death of some of his Katanga Swords—was on a plane, but he had stupidly assumed it was being brought to Chimola's private airstrip. The way N'Kruma reacted told him the plane was en route to some other location where he would not be able to get his hands on it when the time came to depose Chimola.

"Where is the gold?" Lecroix saw the passenger in front of him stir and half turn, eavesdropping. He no longer cared who listened. He felt as if he had the floor dropped from under him and there was a noose around his neck.

"Why bother bringing such a heavy load all the way around the world?" She tried to be flip and deflect his concerns. If anything, she fed them.

"Where?" He wished he had taken the trouble to smuggle his pistol aboard. At the time it had not seemed wise to cirımvent the security at both the U.S. airport and in Mumbai. ·ow he would settle for a knife. Strangling N'Kruma would uell his anger, but explaining the body would be difficult.

"Does it matter? The money will be provided when you eed to buy your…toys."

Lecroix settled back in the seat. The cargo plane traveled ower than a passenger jet. From the spot in the Pacific where e gold would have been unloaded, there were only a few pos-bilities. It came to him in a rush. He gripped the seat arms hard his knuckles turned white. The bitch had sent the gold the Cook Islands and deposited it in a numbered account. witzerland had come under increasing pressure from the EU nd the U.S. to reveal the owners and contents of their banks l too easily. The Cayman Islands were another possibility, ut that was on the far side of the world.

It had to be a numbered account in the Cook Islands.

Tons of gold had just slipped from his grasp unless…

warehouse on Le Beach Ngobila docks, Kinshasa

I WILL DIE FIGHTING!" The rebel with the M-16 stood and egan firing at the Katanga Swords scattered throughout the 'arehouse. The Executioner considered their plight for a oment, then decided the man had the right idea. He stood eside the rebel and began shooting as well. The bass rumble f his Desert Eagle filled the small building with ominous oars every time it discharged.

The .50-caliber pistol along with the rifle was enough to catter the mercs. At least, until they regrouped and formed a ew plan of attack.

"Come on." Bolan shouldered the rebel sideways, and they in for the metal warehouse wall.

"What good is this? It is like one of their firing squads to and here!"

Bolan lowered his shoulder, found what had to be a goo
spot and ran full tilt into the wall. For a horrifying instant, h
thought the wall was too strong. Then he felt something givin
way, and it was not his collarbone. The metal bent outward
then popped free of rusted rivets. Bolan tumbled to the ground
The sound of the rebel's rifle covering his escape continued
giving him hope. He scrambled around on his knees and fire
past the man.

"Get out of there. Where's your car?"

"No good," the rebel said. "The keys are with my drive
My dead driver."

Bolan ejected his pistol's magazine and slammed a new on
in, firing just in time to blow the leg out from under an incau
tious Katanga Swords mercenary. The furor inside warne
that the soldiers would soon recover their wits, and their leade
would set them on the proper trail.

He grabbed the rebel leader and spun him around to fac
the docks.

"Find us a car! Now!" He fired three more times. His deadl
fire forced the Katanga Swords to fall to the concrete an
rethink charging after him. At first the return fire was sporadi
and wild. It settled into a steady hail of death that told him th
mercs had gotten over their confusion and now fought as the
had been trained. And their training looked to be first-rate. On
soldier on either flank advanced, with the center givin
covering fire. Then the flanks opened up and allowed the me
in the middle of the skirmish line to advance. There were to
many for the Executioner to keep firing long. The wall he ha
crashed through now looked like Swiss cheese.

He started to tell the rebel to run for his life when screech
ing tires caught his attention. A car pulled up.

"Your ride," the rebel said, grinning widely. He didn't wai
for Bolan to get into the car before gunning it. Diving throug
the backseat window had been his only way of getting insid

ast enough, but the hard turn caused a four-wheel drift on the pavement and threatened to throw Bolan out. He clung to the ipped seat cover and tore it even more before scrambling ully into the car.

"Where are you going?"

"Take my rifle. Shoot their tires." The rebel raced toward he front of the warehouse where two black SUVs stood, their ngines idling.

Bolan appreciated the man's quick thinking. Why let the Katanga Swords chase them through the crowded streets of a najor city? He used the M-16 until its magazine emptied, hen fired with his own pistol. Four tires had been shot out, efectively crippling the two SUVs. Seeing his passenger's ccurate gunfire, the rebel put the car into a skid again, laying lown more rubber, then accelerated away from the warehouse.

"That wasn't such a safe place, after all," Bolan said.

"Antoine."

"What?"

"I am Antoine."

"It's good to know the name of the man who's going to get ne upriver to Buweh Province," Bolan said. This produced a leep, rich laugh.

"You are the man we thought. You will fight Chimola and ill him."

It sounded so easy. But Bolan knew it would be the fight of his life—and he was ready for it.

15

"Government spies," Antoine said, pointing to a trio of men lounging dockside. "They report immediately to the army if they see any smuggling that is not approved."

"Approved smuggling?" The Executioner had heard stranger things. "Can they be bribed?"

"We do not have enough. We must wait until dark. There is so much activity at the evening tide that they cannot watch everything."

Bolan considered going to the drop point Conrad Quinn had given him to see if the CIA had actually given him a forged passport and other useful items. Even if the CIA intended to throw him to the wolves—or the Katanga Swords—he had to retrieve his own equipment case from the abandoned building where he had stashed it.

He explained his need to Antoine. The rebel shook his head. "It is too dangerous. They will watch and kill you."

"Maybe not," he replied, thinking fast. After explaining what he had in mind, Bolan got a reluctant agreement from the rebel.

"We will do this thing," Antoine said. "But if anything goes wrong, you are on your own."

"Always," the Executioner said. Together they went to find a truck to steal. Along Le Beach Ngobila this proved easy, and they drove from the docks without causing an uproar. Bolan decided the reason the driver, if he had been anywhere nearby when they boosted the truck, had not raised a hue and cry was that he had stolen the vehicle himself, and probably counted himself lucky that the police had not arrested him. The penalty for even minor crimes was severe in the Democratic Republic of the Congo. He had no idea where grand theft auto ranked among the corruption and street rioting.

Bolan let Antoine drive slowly past the boarded-up storefront where he had left his case. The boards appeared to be just like Bolan had left them, so they circled the block once more, passing the store where the van had driven through the window. The owner was there, selling jewelry and other items as if this were nothing more than a convenient teller's window, sliding his wares across a board and taking in payments.

"No one is watching," Antoine said.

Bolan had the feeling this was not true. He ignored obvious tails to concentrate on windows high in buildings across the street. Any number of half-open windows might conceal observers with binoculars, video cameras or even scoped rifles. Movement in a couple windows caught his attention, but nothing alerted him to immediate danger. Still, the way the hairs on the back of his neck rose gave a warning he was unlikely to ignore. He stayed alive relying on his instincts.

"This is going to be quick," Bolan said. "Drop me off and keep driving around the block. When you come back, slow down but don't stop. I'll throw my case into the truck bed and possibly hop back there myself. If I don't, keep driving and we'll rendezvous."

"You do not know the city. How will we meet?" Antoine's voice became shrill with worry. Bolan realized the rebel needed his expertise to fight Chimola, and anything that would prevent that was to be avoided like the plague.

"I'll find you," Bolan said. Antoine looked skeptical, but as he stared hard at the Executioner his doubt faded and he nodded brusquely.

As Antoine slowed, Bolan jumped out of the truck. It sped off, leaving him alone and vulnerable on the sidewalk. He had no reason to think anyone watched this spot—nothing but a feeling in his gut. He went straight for the doorway and leaned heavily against the boards until nails began to pull free with metallic screeches. He twisted and applied his shoulder, not bothering to keep his balance. As he fell, a bullet whined past and kicked up dirt off the interior floor.

Bolan was glad he had trusted his feelings. He kicked and found purchase enough to shove himself deeper into the burned-out store. More bullets came after him, but once he was safely behind brick wall, even the powerful sniper rifle would not reach him. He grabbed his case and opened it. Inside lay some of the most sophisticated electronics available anywhere in the world. All he needed was a short piece of fiber optic cable and the viewer with a small screen that connected to the end.

He slipped it around the door and began a slow study of the building opposite. More than ten minutes passed before the sniper grew anxious and poked his head out to get a better look up and down the street. He ducked back but not before the Executioner got a good look at his face and snapped a picture to send to Stony Man Farm. It hardly mattered if they could identify the sniper, but it gave Kurtzman and the others something for show-and-tell when asked about his progress.

Bolan quickly packed up his case and made his way through the building, being careful not to show himself to the sniper. He kicked out a boarded-up window and spilled onto the adjoining street. Antoine drove by, looking panicky, then relieved when he spotted Bolan.

"Keep driving," the Executioner ordered. "I've got work to do. Meet me at midnight in the warehouse where the Katanga Swords attacked us."

Before Antoine could complain, Bolan was gone. He had replenished his ammo from his case and was ready to go hunting. The sniper was a skeleton of a man who looked as if he had missed most of his meals. But his appearance meant nothing. Bolan had seen snipers of all types. The two things they all had in common were icy nerves and the ability to wait patiently for the right shot. Count heartbeats, wait for the short span between beats, fire, wait for a hit, record it in a kill book.

Cutting across the street, he got to the far side heading in the opposite direction Antoine had driven. He worked his way around, keeping a close watch on the window where he had spotted his adversary. When he was directly under the window, back pressed into the brick wall, he looked up. Again the sniper poked his head out to look up and down the street. Bolan held his breath, fearing the assassin would glance down and spot him. It didn't happen.

He found a doorway into the building and started up the steep flights of rickety stairs. Every time he put his weight down, the wood underneath creaked, threatening to break at any moment. When he reached the second story, he drew his Desert Eagle and went up the final flight of steps more cautiously. Incurious women and children watched him. They had seen killing too many times for a man carrying a pistol, obviously ready to use it, to matter. He was not after them. Therefore, all was as it should be.

The third-floor hall stretched the length of the building, ending in an opened window that let in fresh air and the sounds of traffic. Using the street noise as a cover, he counted down four doors and gently tried the knob. Locked. He stepped back, brought up his foot and kicked. The flimsy door imploded, torn from its hinges. Bolan fired at the movement.

And missed.

He feinted right and dived left in the hall as the powerful Browning .50-caliber round blasted a hole through the wall at waist level. The slug kept going, probably exiting the building after boring holes through more wood and exterior masonry. Rolling, he came to his feet. Pistol aimed at the doorway, he waited. Frightened women looked out from other doors and hastily closed them. None of that distracted him from his vigil. A minute passed. Two. It became a game of endurance.

Then he realized something had to change. He chanced a quick look into the room at floor level, then cursed. He swung around and covered the room in a wide arc. The sniper was gone. Bolan went to the window and looked down. The man had dropped a knotted rope and gone down it, taking his weapon with him. Nowhere was the scrawny man to be seen in the crowds, with or without a gun case.

A thorough search of the room turned up nothing he could use to identify the shooter. The man had perched on a small three-legged stool and watched the burned-out building where Bolan had stashed his case with the patience of a jungle cat waiting for a gazelle to come to the watering hole. He had known how important the case was to Bolan and had counted on his returning.

The Executioner looked over the rushing traffic at the distant doorway on the other side of the street, pointed his index finger, lifted his thumb and quietly said, "Bang." That's how it would have gone down if he had been any less cautious. The sniper knew he could never find Bolan in a city of millions, so he had waited at the only spot where he would have a decent shot.

He left the room, going down the stairs faster than he had mounted them. But he hesitated before exiting to the sidewalk. Again his sense of danger warned him. The sniper had planned an emergency escape route. That meant he had a specific location he considered safe to retreat to. If so, he might have his powerful rifle trained on the door, waiting for Bolan to leave.

Not even chancing a quick glance out, the Executioner found a back door and walked purposefully down an alley, coming out on a side street. He wanted to continue the hunt for the skinny sniper but knew he was at a disadvantage. If he retrieved his case and contacted Stony Man Farm, they might have an identity for him to show Antoine or other rebels. He discarded the notion as he walked, knowing he had more important things to do.

Joseph Chimola. Jacques Lecroix. Pietr Rostov. Perhaps even Coraline N'Kruma. They were the players in a dangerous game of rebellion against a president hardly better than them. He had followed the gold as far as he could. It was time to ignore that and rip out the vile hearts of men intent on overthrowing a government.

The irony of the situation was not lost on the Executioner. He fought to stop a coup that the duly elected government might not even realize existed. He did it without help from the CIA, or perhaps he fought to preserve the government in spite of men like Conrad Quinn. Whatever agenda the CIA had was not likely to match his—or the State Department's.

The thought of the CIA station chief turned his path in other directions. Quinn had said he would leave a new passport and other necessary ID in a drop. Bolan hiked for more than an hour in the steamy atmosphere until he reached the location of the CIA exchange point. After he located a small CCTV camera trained on the spot, it required only seconds for him to yank out the wiring and toss it into the street. Without seeming to hurry, he went to the bench and sat on the far end, near a trash can.

To his surprise, a small package wrapped in filthy canvas dangled behind the can. Bolan snared it and unwrapped the package. Inside lay a U.S. passport made out in the name of Clarence Washington. He smiled at the choice. Never in a thousand years could he have come up with a name like that. Travel papers, a visa and a stack of paper money, all francs, completed the contents.

Bolan carefully studied the passport and other items to be sure Quinn had not bugged anything. If he had, it was more subtle than anything Bolan had ever encountered. He tucked away the contents into a pocket and then saw a scrap of paper stuck to the canvas. "They'll get you up the river better than I could," had been written using a faint pencil. As Bolan held it up to sunlight, the words disappeared and left only a dirty piece of paper.

He had lingered long enough. In a few hours he had to rendezvous with Antoine and begin his trip up the Congo. A final circuit of the area revealed no other cameras or spy devices. That hardly meant Quinn had not extensively wired the entire area, but he had done so more expertly than Bolan could ever detect. He took out the passport and other papers, thought about them for a moment, then tossed them in a trash can some distance from where he had picked them up. Nanowires too small to be seen, RFIDs and other spy devices probably made up the bulk of the passport. The Executioner could get along without being tracked by the CIA.

He headed for Le Beach Ngobila and his transport upriver.

ARRIVING AN HOUR before Antoine, the Executioner waited and watched for anything out of the ordinary. The Katanga Swords would have moved on, hunting in other places for Bolan and the rebels. He had to restrain the urge to hunt them down. Pietr Rostov might also be in Kinshasa by now, leading the search for the man responsible for killing his brother.

A grim smile came to Bolan's lips. The sniper had found bait and had waited. Bolan could use the same technique, dangling himself as bait and waiting for Rostov. As appealing as that was, it was not likely to happen. Eventually, Lecroix had to arrive and draw his PMC around him prior to launching the coup. What the first move would be, Bolan did not know, but it was not going to be in the city. Chimola had to seize and secure the country's interior before squeezing the president militarily and deposing him.

Heavy trucks came and went, moving cargo from the docks.

Semitrucks moved sea containers like those used to ship the stolen gold. He watched them all, imagining every one to be the container he sought. With his case and the detectors inside, he could monitor for the RFID chips.

But the *Spirit of Brazzaville* might not make port here for a month and when it did, there wouldn't be a gram of gold aboard. That was already being airlifted out of Bolan's grasp.

When a Hummer drove by packed with five heavily armed Katanga Swords soldiers in their distinctive uniforms, he pressed back into the shadows and touched the cold butt of his pistol. If there had been only one or two, he would have acted. Information was what he needed more than anything else now, and a prisoner would tell him everything he needed to know. But this many mercs was beyond his reach to capture or kill silently.

The Hummer drove by, the soldiers inside quiet and alert rather than boisterous and unaware. Bolan gave them credit for being well trained. That made the five even less likely to fall victim to a quick attack. They drove on, making Bolan wonder if they patrolled the entire dock area or were on their way to the far end of Le Beach Ngobila where the *Spirit of Brazzaville* would dock eventually. That warehouse supplied not only the Katanga Swords but served as a shipping point for a considerable amount of contraband Chimola brought into the country. The manifests he had found proved that. He only wished he had found out more about the next shipments for Buweh Province.

A gasping, clanking truck came to a halt near the warehouse where Bolan was to meet Antoine. Three men got out and went inside. Gunmetal reflected dully from a distant light. Bolan hurried to a spot behind the truck, chanced a quick look under a tarp and found oilcloth wrapped packages. He pulled one from the truck and slit it open. Rice spilled out. Kicking the white grains into the dirt, he tossed aside the package and poked about the rest and found only supplies.

He worked around to the truck cab and saw a stack of M-16s, boxes of ammo and what might have been cases of hand grenades. Bolan started to pry open one of the crates of explosives when headlights swept around and illuminated him. Like a deer in the headlights, he froze. Then he sank down and pushed the door shut as he drew his pistol.

A car pulled alongside the truck, and Antoine clambered out. Unlike the three from the truck, he dragged out his M-16 and headed for the warehouse with it.

Antoine's pace slowed, and then he stopped. He turned slowly, his M-16 coming up to point in Bolan's direction.

"You know them? Three men got out of this truck."

"I do. They are the river crew. Have you found something?"

"Supplies. Weapons. Explosives."

"Good. They brought everything I asked them for." Antoine lowered his rifle and went into the warehouse, not waiting to see if Bolan followed.

Cautious, the Executioner entered a few seconds after the rebel leader. Antoine and the trio stood to one side, speaking loudly in Lingala. When Antoine pointed over his shoulder, the three saw Bolan for the first time. The one who had carried his rifle from the truck swung it up, but Antoine pushed it aside and spoke angrily.

"It is all right," Antoine called. "They will not harm you."

Bolan knew the rebel had it wrong. He wouldn't kill them.

"Do you have my case?"

"I had to leave the truck. Your case is in the car trunk. We go now." Antoine looked at the three men, who nodded vigorously. "They are eager to return to their village."

Bolan left the warehouse, as anxious to get on the river as the rebels. He went to Antoine's car and jimmied open the trunk. He checked to be sure his case was untouched. Antoine knew what kind of problems would be unleashed if he had tried to open the lid and had done nothing to compromise the contents. Bolan stuffed the handful of Democratic Republic of the Congo francs into his coat pocket where he could get to them quickly if a bribe was needed.

"We go," Antoine said. He jumped into the rear of the pickup truck. The other three already crowded into the cab, leaving the rear for Bolan. He tossed in his case and climbed in as they roared off.

"We will take a boat home—to Buweh," Antoine said.

"How long have you been in Kinshasa?" Bolan gripped the edge of the truck as they raced toward the waterfront. They were close enough for the sound of water lapping against the docks to be audible, along with the other peculiar noises of river travel. When the stench of dead fish became almost overpowering, the truck veered and drove parallel to the Congo River.

"I have been in the city too long. Almost three years," Antoine said. "I came to attend the university but did not graduate."

"Politics?"

"I began to protest the president. I protested even more when he appointed Chimola as governor of my home province." He turned morose. "The more I protested, the worse the situation became. Now I know. Parades and protests mean nothing to a well-aimed rifle." Antoine held up his M-16.

The truck turned abruptly and bounced down a rocky shore to where a small boat was moored. The rude dock was obviously not part of commercial shipping at Le Beach Ngobila. When it stopped, Bolan and Antoine vaulted out and began helping to unload the truck.

"The food is more than we need for the trip," Antoine explained. "Chimola starves villagers to coerce cooperation. We will feed them and win their support."

Bolan hoped this would happen, but he didn't put much hope in it as a way of winning a guerrilla war. Chimola held all the trump cards. That meant the Executioner had to stack the deck against him.

"We are ready," Antoine said, strapping down the last of the supplies.

"All is moved," said another of the rebels. Then he abruptly died with a bullet in the back of his head.

Bolan drew his pistol as a dozen more bullets came singing through the night, boring holes in the boat and killing another of the rebels.

16

N'Dgili International Airport, Kinshasa

Jacques Lecroix pressed his cheek against the cold plastic window to watch the ground rushing up. The jumbo jet touched down without so much as a bump, then deceleration pushed him against his seat belt and finally back again as the plane slowed to a halt.

"Are you happy to return?" Coraline N'Kruma said, mocking him.

"I want to get to work," he said, not bothering to turn toward her. He wondered if Nogomo could remove her with a single shot without causing Chimola to react too badly. If her death appeared random, Chimola would be angry for a while, then would return to his schemes for taking over the country. Perhaps he might plant evidence that the president of the Democratic Republic of the Congo was responsible for N'Kruma's murder, but to do this without suspicion falling on his own head required some planning. And there was no time. No time before the coup got underway.

"Always the soldier," she said. "Joseph must be proud of you."

"Does he know you diverted the gold to a numbered account in the Cook Islands?"

"I am a financier," she said with a touch of ice in her tone now. "You deal with the—what do you call it? Wet work. I will handle the monetary concerns."

"Fondle the gold, you mean," Lecroix grumbled.

The plane swung about and taxied to the terminal. Lecroix was on his feet and heading down the jetway before N'Kruma gathered her carry-on luggage. He preferred to travel light to clear security and customs quickly.

"One moment, Jacques," she called.

N'Kruma hurried along to catch up, looking flustered for the first time since he had known she was accompanying him to the United States for the gold thefts.

"We must not squabble. Mutual understanding will make both our jobs easier." She touched her lips with the tip of her tongue, tentatively making a play for him. A dozen sharp replies were born and died in his brain.

"We must focus our skills," he said. "You are right."

"Of course I am," she said, smiling now. She looped her arm through his as they went to the baggage area.

Customs went quickly when the agent saw they were both listed as being on Provincial Governor Chimola's staff. Four Katanga Swords soldiers waited to take the luggage and escort Lecroix and N'Kruma to the stretch Hummer limo where Pietr Rostov paced like a caged animal.

"It's about time," Rostov said. "You are back."

"Yes, we are," N'Kruma said easily. She went to Rostov and kissed him lightly on both cheeks while Lecroix watched. The play of emotion on Rostov's face was informative. N'Kruma had to have seduced the dour Russian. Lecroix fumed at this betrayal. If only he had the account number and password of the Cook Islands account, N'Kruma would feed the crocodiles with her svelte body.

If only…

"Are we ready to go to Buweh?" Lecroix watched as Rostov stepped away from the woman and stood at attention.

"Sir, the boat is at the docks. We can be on the river in less than an hour."

Lecroix nodded curtly and motioned for N'Kruma to enter the mo. She held out her hand for him to aid her. He considered hat he needed from her and decided that making her an enemy, r more of an enemy, would not serve his purposes. With a slight od in her direction, he helped her into the vehicle. From the orner of his eye he saw Rostov's reaction and wondered when e whore had seduced his second in command. Before entering fter her, Lecroix turned and put his hand on Rostov's shoulder.

"We will avenge your brother's murder," he said softly. "Is ere any news on who was responsible?"

"Only rumors. It was a white man, tall, probably American."

Lecroix nodded and climbed into the limo. He wished he ad not killed the spy aboard the *Spirit of Brazzaville*. Finding ho he worked for and the extent of the U.S. opposition would e useful to know now. Then he turned his thoughts to more nportant matters. He had a revolution to lead and a puppet put into charge of an entire country.

Then he would loot every franc, every pound, every dollar nd euro from the Democratic Republic of the Congo's banks efore finding a nice spot in South America to retire. It would e nice to add the Cook Islands gold to his hoard, but there would e time to deal with Coraline N'Kruma later. After Chimola ssumed the presidency and confusion and terror reigned.

HE EXECUTIONER SQUEEZED off a shot, killing a man with a achine gun. He fired rapidly into the dark bank of the Congo iver, missing with the other shots but causing enough conusion among the attackers that Antoine was able to bark out ommands and get the handful of his rebels into the fight.

"Who attacks?"

Bolan didn't care who shot at them. It could be the Katanga words or the police or even some other rebel group wanting hijack the food and weapons Antoine had loaded onto the otorboat. What he wanted was to remove the threat and get away from Kinshasa. He observed how Antoine arrayed the two men remaining to him and where their field of fire lay. Skirting the battlefield, he circled and came at the attackers from their left flank. His gun spit death. The man collapsed without making a sound.

Scooping up the dead man's machine gun, Bolan turned it on the remaining tight knot of attacking soldiers. He fired until the gun jammed. Rather than clear it, he tossed the weapon to his left, drawing fire away from him. The orange tongue of flame leaping from another of the soldiers' weapons drew Bolan's more accurate fire. When the Executioner shot, he killed. This death caused some consternation in the attackers' ranks, making him think he had taken out their commanding officer.

Bolan charged, firing on the run. The soldiers broke and retreated. He shot at the remaining five men, wounding one. The rest vanished into the night. Bolan hurried to the wounded man's side and pointed his pistol directly between the frightened man's eyes.

"I will kill him!" Antoine pushed Bolan to the side and moved to kill their prisoner.

"Wait." He knelt, his knee in the supine man's belly. "Who sent you? Who do you work for? You're all wearing army uniforms."

"The president. We are the president's elite river guard!"

"Elite," Antoine scoffed. "They are pirates. They kill and steal boats and supplies, then sell them on the black market."

"They're not with the Katanga Swords," Bolan said. He felt the man pinned by his knee squirm at the mention of the PMC. "What do you know about the Katanga Swords?"

"Nothing. I know nothing—!" The soldier gasped for breath as Bolan pressed down harder. When the man began to pass out, the big American eased off. The sound of the air going back into his prisoner's lungs sounded like a furnace bellow.

"What about the Katanga Swords?"

"We work with them but not tonight. They all go to the airport."

"Why?"

"Their commander returns. At N'Dgili. They are to escort Lecroix upriver to Buweh tonight."

"And you hijack cargo," Antoine said.

Bolan felt the prisoner jerk as the rebel leader's bullet ripped through his heart. He pushed back to his feet and looked at the corpse.

"Gather their weapons. Every gun and bullet matters," Bolan said.

"You do not approve. He could tell us nothing more," Antoine said.

"What I think has nothing to do with it. He was a soldier and worked for the government."

Antoine nodded once, his fierce expression telling more than words. The rebels hated the president and his army for not quelling Chimola's atrocities. Given the chance, Antoine and his countrymen would overthrow the elected president as well as putting down Joseph Chimola. So much for the enemy of his enemy being an ally. In the Democratic Republic of the Congo, everyone shot at everyone else.

The Executioner's mission was to stop Chimola. If a new revolt brewed in Buweh and other provinces after he eliminated the governor, that was someone else's problem. Let Conrad Quinn handle that new can of worms. For all he knew, the CIA had already considered the possibilities and promises and was acting on them.

"Pierre is wounded," Antoine said. He helped the man with a bullet in his side aboard the boat. "He must steer, since he is only pilot we have."

"Is the way that treacherous?" Bolan looked out at the swiftly flowing Congo. A river this powerful required skills he did not have to drive the boat if it got caught in a tricky current.

"In places, closer to Chimola's checkpoints," Antoine assured him. The rebel leader gestured and the other man threw off the bowline. Bolan jumped into the boat, causing it to rock precariously as the stern line was dropped and the boat responded to the powerful current.

He settled down, a captured machine gun in his grip as he watched the receding shoreline. The soldiers were probably still running, but eventually they would tire and figure out some cock-and-bull story about an entire company of smugglers ambushing them. Anything that got them off the hook and free of punishment for being so inept. When the officer in charge found the bodies of his men, all hell would break loose.

The boat's engine sputtered and coughed, but it kept running. Pierre leaned over the wheel, making adjustments to their course that took them almost to the middle of the channel where the current ran strongest. Bolan abandoned his watch and went to the pilot. He placed a forefinger against the man's throat.

"Antoine, he's dead."

Antoine came forward. He verified Bolan's diagnosis, threw his arms around the man's waist and heaved him away from the wheel.

"You steer." Antoine said nothing more as he grunted and cursed, dragging Pierre's body to the side and tossing it over. The rebel bobbed in the current a moment and then vanished in the dark, muddy flow.

Bolan angled toward the far side of the river, cutting across the main shipping lane. That side belonged to the Congo Republic, and there wasn't likely to be any soldiers looking to shoot them out of the water. Or so he thought until Antoine came forward and nudged him.

"Back," was all Antoine said. Bolan saw the danger. Soldiers had set up an M-249 SAW on the bank and worked to load it. Since their boat was the only target in sight, Bolan knew they had to get out of range fast.

"I wanted to steer clear of the soldiers who ambushed us," he said.

"All soldiers along the river, either bank, know we are smugglers. They want our contraband and will kill to get it," Antoine said.

"How far is it to Buweh?" Bolan maneuvered the boat back through the fastest running section of the Congo and eventually came within twenty yards of the bank belonging to the Democratic Republic of the Congo again.

"Two days, maybe three," Antoine said. The engine missed a stroke, causing the boat to lurch. "Or longer."

Bolan settled down for what was likely to be a long and dangerous trip.

"THE LAUNCH IS READY, sir," Rostov said. "We have fuel and supplies."

"Very well," Jacques Lecroix said. He stepped into the powerful motor launch and began a quick examination. While he usually trusted Rostov, the man's behavior had been erratic recently. More than the death of Andre gnawed at his black Russian soul, and Lecroix had to figure out what it might be before he was assured of the man's abilities. It likely had to do with some notion N'Kruma had planted in his brain.

As he counted the jerricans of diesel fuel, he saw Rostov and N'Kruma talking. She pressed close to Rostov, but the Russian appeared uncomfortable at her nearness. N'Kruma spoke rapidly and too low for Lecroix to overhear.

"Cast off!" Lecroix barked, and two of his soldiers obeyed. The sudden lurch as the boat slipped away from the dock and was caught by the inexorable flow of the Congo River caused Rostov and N'Kruma to fall together. The Russian's hand went around the small of her back in a way that appeared all too familiar. Knowing his commander watched, Rostov backed away quickly, as if the woman's skin burned his hand.

Whatever was between the two bore careful examination. Lecroix turned from that problem and made a final inspection of the rest of the motor launch. Whether Rostov had made certain it was shipshape or one of the other Katanga Swords had done so, he approved. Lecroix made a point of speaking with each of the six soldiers accompanying them on the trip to Buweh.

"We will be on the river only two days, eh?"

"Yes, sir," the pilot said, standing at attention as he threaded the sleek boat between others along the busy dock area.

"To Buweh," Lecroix went on. "Both province and capital city share the same name. They must not have any imagination."

The soldier grinned when he realized Lecroix joked. "They will name the town after you when we win."

"Or after you, if you fight bravely," Lecroix said, slapping the man on the shoulder. "Keep up the good work." He walked away and joined N'Kruma and Rostov at the stern where they watched the foam from the twin propellers melt into the dark water of the Congo.

"Will the tanks be delivered soon?" he asked N'Kruma.

"Should I know?"

"You control the purse strings," Lecroix said more to watch Rostov's reaction than to anger the woman. He was not disappointed. Rostov jumped as if he had been jabbed with a knife in the back.

"You exaggerate. I took care of only the...one item."

"Five or six tons of gold is so little to you? To me, it is the success of the revolution. With even a single tank, chances of victory increase. Surely, you can release some of the millions in that numbered account."

Rostov stalked off without a word.

"It is not wise to speak of such things in front of the hired hands," N'Kruma said. "They do not understand how expensive it is to wage war, even in a backward country like this."

"There are always great costs," Lecroix said.

N'Kruma followed Rostov below, leaving Lecroix alone. He drew out his cell phone and quickly dialed.

"Yes?" came the immediate response.

"Go to Buweh and prepare," Lecroix said.

"How many?"

"There will be two," Lecroix said. "Possibly a third, though that is not clear at the moment. Why do you ask, Nogomo? Are you getting squeamish?"

"I failed to get him. The tall American. He is very good, and he still roams Kinshasa."

"You missed him?" This took Lecroix by surprise. Nogomo never missed once his target was sighted in.

"He anticipated me. That is not good."

"Forget the American and go immediately to the town. Do you need more money?"

"No." Nogomo hung up, leaving Lecroix with a dead phone to his ear.

He thumbed it off, then heaved it as hard as he could into the river. It had only been a cheap Indian knockoff of a good phone, but he had used it too many times. Let the CIA hunt for it now.

Lecroix looked toward the shore and saw a small boat struggling along. He grinned without humor. Smugglers. They were the lifeblood of the Democratic Republic of the Congo, supplying goods the government could not. Chimola had alliances with many of them to prepare for his coup in Kinshasa, but Lecroix knew they would turn on the governor in a heartbeat if someone offered them more money. Threatening their lives meant nothing and would never motivate them or command their loyalty. They risked their necks every time they put out in their flimsy boats and dealt with rebels and soldiers alike. Only money drove them.

Only money. That thought rattled about in Lecroix's head as he went below to join Rostov and N'Kruma.

"THE ENGINE DOESN'T sound too good," Bolan said.

"Molo has kept it running for a month now. He will, as you say, goose it all the way to Buweh."

Bolan didn't share Antoine's confidence in the mechanic. Molo used the hammer and a wrench more to bang on the faltering engine than to fix it, yet it never quite died, even if it also did not purr like a contented kitten.

"How likely are we to be fired on from the shore?" Bolan's keen eyes had picked up several small groups of men skulking along the river. More than once he was certain he saw a rifle or machine gun in their hands.

"Very likely," Antoine said. "They live off the wrecked smugglers."

"Scavengers," Bolan said. He preferred those who fought their own battles rather than picking the carcasses left behind, yet scavengers had a purpose. Even as that thought crossed his mind, he responded to movement onshore. The Executioner lifted his machine gun and let out a staccato burst that raked the tree line. A single answering shot went wide.

"Don't waste ammunition on them," Antoine said.

Bolan did not want yet another hole in the boat's hull. When Molo wasn't working on the engine, he bailed water to keep them from going under. Antoine did what he could to navigate as he stood on the darkened prow, yelling back directions to Bolan on avoiding swiftly moving tree limbs. Some of the things in the water he missed looked like human bodies. More than once he saw a shadowy log moving with the current, only to suddenly dart toward shore and vanish beneath the surface. Antoine did not have to tell him the waters were infested with hungry crocodiles that sometimes ventured into swift running water before returning to their more peaceful stagnant swamps away from the river.

Scavengers, both human and reptilian. Bolan touched his Desert Eagle and then put both hands back on the steering wheel.

The roar of a powerful launch overtaking them made him

steer closer to the shore. The thirty-two-foot launch zoomed past twenty yards toward the center of the river. At the stern a man turned and threw something into the river. He stood stock-still, making Bolan think he watched the rebels' small boat. Then the shadowy figure disappeared, going belowdeck. Within a minute, the boat had left the rebel craft far behind.

Bolan watched as the power launch disappeared into the night, a feeling in his gut that he had just missed something and did not know what.

17

Buweh Province, Democratic Republic of the Congo

Jacques Lecroix jumped from the boat to the dock before it had been moored securely, hurrying to the SUV that waited for him. He hesitated, then swung into the front seat beside the driver and said, "To the palace immediately."

"Sir, the others—"

"Now!"

The driver looked at Coraline N'Kruma and Pietr Rostov hurrying along the dock, but Lecroix grabbed the wheel and jerked on it.

"Drive!"

The chauffeur accelerated smoothly onto the road and sped along at better than seventy miles per hour in spite of the rough road. Lecroix hardly noticed how he was bounced about. He was lost in thought about what he would say to Joseph Chimola before the others could seize his attention. The man needed to be warned about N'Kruma and possibly even Rostov, but the Russian could be taken care of. Lecroix would do that himself if the need arose. For the moment, he still had a use for Rostov, even if he and Coraline N'Kruma had begun plotting against him and Chimola.

"We're here, sir."

Lecroix paid the driver no attention. He was out the door and hurrying inside before the SUV had stopped rolling. The house was an old French colonial mansion that Chimola had renovated after it had stood empty for more than forty years. Now it was truly a palace. The Italian marble floors just inside the tall double doors opening into the foyer gleamed in reflected light so fierce that Lecroix squinted. He turned to his left—Chimola's study. He had to say his piece before Coraline N'Kruma showed up, or Chimola would be brought back under her charms again from nothing more than her presence.

The fool!

"Commander, welcome back."

"Sir," Lecroix said, closing the study door behind him. He felt the man's magnetic personality, the power of his smile and the way he seemed to empathize. This was Joseph Chimola, the politician. Lecroix preferred Chimola the soldier—he was more logical and ruthless.

"Where are the others?"

"Taking another car," Lecroix said. "I need to discuss an urgent matter with you before they arrive."

"I have no secrets from Coraline," Chimola said.

"She does from you, sir. She has placed the gold stolen in a numbered account."

"In the Cook Islands," Chimola said, frowning. "Do you believe she would not tell me this?"

"She didn't tell me and—"

"There was no need, Commander," Chimola said. His voice turned to ice, and his friendly demeanor changed. "You overstep your bounds."

"I only meant for you to know and to transfer the money to a Kinshasa bank."

"Before the coup? No, it is safer out of the country, Commander," Chimola said. "You need not concern yourself with such matters. Put in requisitions for arms and I will have them filled with the gold you have provided. Brilliant work, Commander, stealing under the cover of a forest fire." Chimola laughed, deep and resonant. "Such could never happen in this country. The jungle is far too wet."

"There is more I need to warn you about, sir—" Lecroix said.

"Ah, come in, my dear. Rostov, go muster the troops. I am sure your commander will want to see them in review."

Lecroix sucked in his breath and held it for a moment, letting it out slowly to control his anger. Coraline N'Kruma crossed the room in her easy model's catwalk glide and kissed Chimola, then stood hip to hip with him, arm around his waist. The smirk on her lips made Lecroix want to kill her then and there.

"What more did you want to report, Commander?"

Lecroix looked the governor squarely in the eye and lied.

THE EXECUTIONER SIGHTED down the rifle barrel as the boat silently slipped closer to the first of Chimola's security checkpoints on the river. Twilight turned the jungle lining the riverbanks into a thing alive. Through the thick undergrowth moved smaller animals, stalked by larger ones. Crocs wiggled into the water and turned into logs more deadly than anything else, except for the soldiers in the towers on either side of the river.

Bolan worried more about the observation tower on the far bank because the guard had a good view of the bank where Antoine's boat edged forward. The nearer tower's field of view was limited downward, giving them a chance to sneak by it in the dark. He had turned his rifle upward, putting a soldier in his sights when the sentry yelled across the river to his counterpart.

Tense, wondering what the soldiers were shouting about, Bolan watched as the tower slipped behind and the boat continued on, unseen.

Then all hell broke loose. An alarm went off and sun-bright spotlights began sweeping the river. Bolan held off firing.

"Motion sensors," Antoine said. "They are usually broken. Bad luck they work now."

"Keep going. Something else might have set off the alarm." Bolan swiveled around, wondering if he ought to take out the more distant guard first. He swung back, covering the guard in the tower now twenty yards behind them. The spotlights centered on the middle of the river, well away from the boat. By the time they rounded a bend into a narrower stretch of the river, Bolan saw that a large log floating in the strong current had set off the alarm.

"They ought to be more vigilant," Bolan said, relaxing. "It's ridiculous to set their sensors for the middle of the river. How long before we get to Buweh?"

"We are in the province now. The city is a bit more than twenty yards ahead."

Bolan had tried to contact Stony Man Farm to learn of the gold shipment and Lecroix's location, but the heavy foliage along the banks had blocked satellite communication. He was less worried about Chimola intercepting the link than he was the CIA listening in, but his inability to make any contact put him on his own.

Still, he could have used some aerial recon photos of the surrounding jungle. As they made their way upriver, he heard powerful engines out in the jungle, hidden from sight by heavy foliage. Some he identified by their sound as APCs. Occasional small-arms fire punctuated the mechanized travel but otherwise he had no idea what went on.

The patrol boat caught them by surprise. A spotlight clicked on and fixed on the bow an instant before a light machine gun opened up. Bolan jerked away instinctively, hitting the deck and grabbing for his rifle.

Antoine spun, blood spraying from his arm. Molo, fighting at the engine to get more speed, was hit and died instantly.

"Overboard," Bolan ordered. He laid down covering fire for

Antoine. His first round took out the spotlight. The second caused someone on the patrol boat to scream in pain. After emptying the magazine, he dropped the rifle, grabbed a machine gun and followed Antoine overboard just as a fiery trail of an RPG snaked through the night and struck the boat's superstructure. For a moment, the rocket grenade only sizzled and sprayed sparks, then erupted with a flare that blasted fifty feet into the air. Bolan kicked hard and shot through the water until he reached the muddy bank. He got to his feet, then half-dragged Antoine into the thicket where they lay panting from the exertion and their near brush with death. Their boat burned down to the waterline, then sank within seconds.

"That was close," Bolan said. He made a quick inventory of his equipment. Almost everything had gone to the bottom of the river with the boat, but he still had his Desert Eagle with a few spare magazines, the machine gun and his grim determination to finish his mission.

"Yes," Antoine rasped.

Bolan went to work cleaning and bandaging the rebel's wound as best he could. The bullet had gone through the man's upper left biceps, leaving the arm useless. In his right hand, Antoine gripped a pistol with all the intensity Bolan felt.

"We must go," Antoine said. "They will search for bodies, and a single one will not satisfy them. They won't believe the crocs ate us so quickly."

The Executioner helped Antoine to his feet. They followed a faint path through the jungle and suddenly came out onto a dirt road running parallel to the river. He turned in the direction they had been sailing and listened. Ahead he heard machinery, men and what sounded like the preparation for a war.

He grabbed Antoine and shoved him off the road as a truck, headlights glaring onto the road, lumbered up from behind them. The Executioner waited for it to pass, then ran along behind a few paces and pulled himself into the rear of the APC.

He wasted no time getting to the front of the troop compartment and peered through a tiny window. Only the driver sat up front. Bolan drew his pistol and thrust it through the small window so the muzzle pressed into the man's ear.

The driver jumped and swerved, causing the APC to crash into a tree. The impact sent the driver up and through the windshield so his head poked completely through the glass. He kicked feebly a moment, then died as he bled out from his neck wounds. Bolan wasted no time getting around to the driver's door. He yanked it open, got in and clumsily kicked out the windshield. By that time Antoine had pulled himself into the passenger seat.

"What do we do?"

"Explore," Bolan said. He wiped off some blood from the steering wheel and got the APC into gear. That it was empty meant the driver had been sent to pick up a squad and deliver the soldiers somewhere downriver. He asked Antoine what lay behind and got a grim answer.

"My village, my people. They have resisted Chimola from the day he was appointed governor."

"Chimola is launching his coup." Bolan remembered the river and knew the places where Chimola would put up his new checkpoints to strangle river trade. The existing stations would be only the start. By the time he was done, the governor would have cut off all transport to the river and nothing would move on the Congo without his permission.

"I must go to them," Antoine said.

"First we reconnoiter to know what we're up against."

"It is only the two of us. We cannot stop the assault now."

"No, the two of us can't." Bolan saw a line of trucks ahead and slipped out of the driver's seat as he motioned for Antoine to take his place. Two of them couldn't stop a revolution.

But one could if it was the Executioner.

"Turn around and return to your village. Prepare them

however you can. I'd suggest hiding in the jungle and fighting like guerrillas."

"What are you going to do?"

Bolan did not answer. He was already focused on the job ahead.

"PIETR IS RIGHT," Coraline N'Kruma said, coming around the desk in the study of the governor's palace. "Jacques has become unstable. Perhaps it was his carousing in America with the whores and dope addicts. I don't know the reason, but he has become obsessed with keeping the gold needed to finance your coup."

"I cannot believe this," Joseph Chimola said, shaking his head. "Lecroix is a fine commander. The Katanga Swords is the best PMC in Africa." He looked at Pietr Rostov. "You agree with her?"

"I do," Pietr Rostov said. "Lecroix has not been efficient. He has allowed American agents to best him twice."

"CIA?" Chimola asked.

"Who else would it be, dearest?" N'Kruma said. "He claims to have killed one in San Francisco on the *Spirit of Brazzaville* just before it left the harbor, but I doubt he actually succeeded. Another has been nosing about Kinshasa and was seen leaving the American Embassy. Lecroix has done nothing about him, either."

"But such treachery as you describe goes beyond mere incompetence."

"A mistake now means defeat, Joseph," she said softly, her hand moving slowly up and down his arm.

"I can command the Katanga Swords. Let me eliminate Lecroix." Rostov looked from N'Kruma to Chimola as he puffed out his broad chest.

"This is the account number in the Cook Islands?" Chimola

eld up a scrap of paper. "If I contact them, they will release ie gold without question?"

"Of course, my dear," N'Kruma said.

"Very well. Remove Lecroix however you see fit. You are ie new commander, Rostov. And you, my lovely, we must iscuss this in…more depth."

"In your bedroom?" N'Kruma smiled wickedly. "It will be iy pleasure."

"No, Coraline, it will be mine," Chimola said. Together they ·ft the study and went up the broad steps to the second floor. ostov waited a moment, then hurriedly left.

After the outer door closed, Jacques Lecroix peered into the oom from his hiding place behind a row of filing cabinets. He eethed that Rostov thought he would make a better com-iander of the Katanga Swords. Lecroix had trained them per-onally! Each was handpicked and honed like the finest blade or battle.

He drew out a cell phone and pressed a speed dial button.

"Yes?"

"The woman," he said.

"The other, also?"

"Not yet," Lecroix said. The phone went dead. He replaced in his pocket, knowing Nogomo would swiftly eliminate 'Kruma. There might be a way to salvage the rest of his lans, but they depended on Chimola overthrowing the gov-rnment in Kinshasa. So many banks to loot. So much wealth.

The image of the paper with the account number on it urned in his mind, but not as brightly as seeing Rostov egging to live just before his life was snuffed out. Lecroix lenched his fingers into hard fists and relaxed only when ain from his fingernails cutting into his own flesh warned him iat he was to deliver agony, not inflict it on himself.

He left the governor's palace and went after Rostov.

The Executioner had seen many military operations an gauged that the Katanga Swords inside the chain-link fence compound were almost ready to begin a full-scale attack. Th heavy trucks were lined up, ready to transport squads into th field. Some artillery stood to one side of the large clearing, bu there was no evidence of their being moved yet. The soldier marched in neat ranks and their noncoms made certain thei equipment was in combat readiness. Whatever Chimo planned depended entirely on ground troops and surprise.

As he skirted the compound, something did not seem righ to him. He finally figured it out. The open field where th Katanga Swords assembled was too dark. Looking up hig above the equipment, Bolan spotted camo nets stretched out designed to prevent any aerial observation. From the intricat design and the odd power leads coming off the netting, h guessed there was some sort of built-in electric field intende to block satellite recon, too. The satellites lofted by the NRO NSA and others in the spy community used more than simpl visual observation to detect movement. Infrared could follow individual soldiers and synthetic aperture radar actually looke below the ground. The netting was a high-tech way of blockin out even the most sophisticated space spying, and the cam pattern confused casual aerial observation.

He studied the way the corners of the netting ran into bat teries and guessed it required a considerable amount of juic o keep the screen functioning properly. Working his way around, the Executioner found a spot where he could dig under he chain-link fence. Once inside, he quietly walked to one of he few permanent buildings inside the fence. The traditional kull-and-crossbones sign on the shed told him something iseful was likely kept inside. The door was heavily barred and adlocked. Bolan circled the building and noted an area where ome small creature had already begun burrowing under the uilding. He quickly enlarged the hole so he could fit through, and within a few minutes he popped a board up out of the floor and got inside.

Explosives of all kinds were stacked from floor to ceiling. He found a sack and began loading it with blocks of C-4, letonators and a radio transmitter capable of setting them off.

For good measure Bolan added a few hand grenades. He ushed the heavily laden sack ahead of him and came out— only to see a sentry patrolling not ten feet away.

The guard stopped and turned, looking out into the jungle on he far side of the fence. He swung around his AK-47 and walked closer. As he reached for his flashlight to see what was making noise outside the perimeter, the Executioner moved. He covered he distance between them in a flash. His right arm circled the guard's neck and dragged him back onto his heels as a sharp knife drove up and into the man's heart from behind. The guard gave a convulsive kick, and without uttering a sound he died. Bolan eased him to the ground and searched him. The walkie-talkie would be useful for listening in to the command channel.

He took the AK-47 and a pouch of magazines as well as a Beretta carried in a holster. Bolan dragged the guard's body back, crammed it into the hole under the shed, then hefted his bag of explosives and went to the fence.

The Executioner placed a block of C-4, a cap and an electronic detonator in every spot where electrical leads came down to batteries. He made sure he saved a few blocks of the explosive as he went to the fuel dump. By the looks of their rudimentary motor pool, this was a staging area, not a permanent base. But the diesel and gasoline in drums would be a perfect flare in the night. He set his charges and took out the transmitter, flicking his thumb back and forth over the safety.

But Bolan wanted to be outside the compound when he set off his fireworks. As the Executioner headed for the hole under the fence he heard a ruckus—and two familiar voices. He had to blow the place soon or the mercs and their equipment would be moved out, but having both Rostov and Lecroix was an opportunity he could not pass up.

He slung his captured assault rifle and marched off, as if he had every right in the world to be inside the compound. The few Katanga Swords who passed by never glanced in his direction. As he got closer to a darkened tent near the far end of the compound, he just barely made out Pietr Rostov through the opening and he clearly heard Jacques Lecroix's voice.

"You sold me out to that bitch," Lecroix said.

"You betrayed him. You betrayed Chimola!" Rostov moved around, hand resting on his holstered sidearm.

Bolan could end their argument for them with a quick burst from the Russian weapon. He hefted it and jacked in a round as he approached.

"She uses you. She uses him for her own purposes. She stole the gold!"

"No, Lecroix, she didn't. She gave Chimola the account number."

Bolan slowed his approach. Learning the account number would go a long way toward recovering it for Marshal Phillips.

"How do you know it is all the gold? She might have split it into many accounts and given Chimola only a small one to keep him from suspecting," Lecroix said.

"She wouldn't."

"You're a fool, Rostov. She is evil and would do anything for power."

"Like you?"

"You know my plans. Every man in the Katanga Swords will be rich when we loot the Kinshasa banks. To hell with Chimola after that. What does he care for any of us? We're hired servants, nothing more. Why is your loyalty to him and not to me, to the Katanga Swords? Pietr, we are partners, you and I."

"You want it all, and you had my brother killed because he learned of your plans."

"What?" Lecroix sounded genuinely confused.

"Andre knew your real plan. You were going to kill us all when you got the money. By remaining loyal to Chimola, I can be his right-hand man, and not your lackey."

Suddenly Bolan was dazzled by the flash from a pistol in the dark. He didn't know who had shot it, but that hardly mattered to him. He pulled back on the trigger and emptied the magazine in the direction of the tent.

"Intruders! Someone shot Rostov!" Lecroix came from the tent, pistol firing wildly. The Executioner rammed in another magazine and emptied it at the leader of the Katanga Swords, but missed. From the report of the SIG-Sauer and the length of the muzzle-flash, he guessed Lecroix had killed Rostov and now tried to kill him. From what he had overheard of their argument, the woman had successfully driven a wedge between the two mercenaries. Andre Rostov's death at the Executioner's hand might have contributed to Pietr's paranoia.

The Katanga Swords' officers had been drilling their men and had them honed for combat. They simply loosed them sooner than they had expected. Unfortunately, they were set on Bolan. He fired until he ran out of ammo for the AK-47 and drew the Beretta, wishing now he had taken spare rounds for it. He fired methodically, being sure of his target before squeezing the trigger. The sound of his stolen weapon merged with others of the same model and gave him a small measure of cover.

That would not last long. He worked his way toward the chain-link fence, pulled out the transmitter and pushed back the safety guard. His thumb crushed the tiny red button, causing a needle on a meter to swing wildly.

The explosions cutting through the netting supports overhead were nothing compared with the ground-shaking roar as the fuel dump erupted in flame. Bolan turned from the intense heat, then looked back at the inferno. He knew he had failed to get Lecroix. The man had been running when he left the command tent after killing Rostov. By the time the explosion went off, he would have reached the trucks.

Bolan skirted the worst of the fire and saw that, for all the flash, there was little destruction. The Katanga Swords had withstood the flaming net falling on them, since it was little more than nylon mesh. Some might have received minor burns, but very few were incapacitated. Looking at the line of trucks, he saw where one had pulled out.

Before the PMC officers could get control of their men again, Bolan walked through the confusion. He grabbed one man and shook him hard enough to rattle his teeth.

"Where's Commander Lecroix?"

"Truck," the soldier said, his eyes glassy with shock.

"Carry on," Bolan said and ran off, looking in every truck he came to until he found one with keys in the ignition. He didn't have time to hot-wire a truck—stealing one ready to roll was easier. As he slid into the cab, two Katanga Swords soldiers trotted up, rifles at port arms.

"Who're you?"

"Going after Lecroix," he called. Bolan reached across and drew his Desert Eagle, ready for a fight. It came fast. The soldiers exchanged looks, then one turned and began firing at him. His handgun's fire drowned out the reports of their

AK-47, and with four shots he took out both soldiers. Putting the truck into gear, Bolan drove away. As he rolled past the guard at the gate leading into the compound, he yelled out his question about Lecroix's whereabouts.

"He went to the governor's palace," came the reply. Bolan roared past.

The rough road pounded him hard, but he refused to slow. His headlights lanced out and caught the edges of jungle trying to reclaim the rutted lane. The farther he drove, the narrower the road became. He was glad of one thing. Wherever Lecroix had gone, he had not taken an easily missed side road.

After more than fifteen minutes of breakneck driving, he saw taillights ahead. Bolan kept up the pace and closed on the other truck. It didn't matter that the truck ahead slammed on its brakes. He rammed into it. Even if the other driver had not stopped, Bolan would have collided to knock the other vehicle off the road. Locked together, bumper-to-bumper, the two heavy trucks skewed off the road and plowed into the heavy jungle growth. For an instant, Bolan thought his truck might stay on its wheels, but then it tipped precariously and flopped over. He braced himself against the top of the cab as the vehicle rolled.

Turning painfully, he got his feet under him, jumping up and out the window on the passenger side. He spun around, then sat, feet dangling down into the cab so he could look around. The other truck was mired in mud. Its wheels spun. Spinning wheels meant the driver was still inside. Bolan drew his pistol, dropped to the jungle floor and stalked forward.

He circled the other truck and fired when he saw a silhouette against the windshield. Glass shattered, but he knew he had missed. The driver ducked.

"Lecroix!"

No answer. Bolan moved closer and then was hurled backward as the door exploded. Shrapnel whined past his head and lacerated his arms and upper body. He fell back heavily and lay waiting. He ached, but the wounds from the hand grenade were nothing if he could get a good shot at Lecroix.

The man did not come after him. Bolan heard noises on the far side of the truck, got to his feet and then ran the best he could. He braced his gun hand against the hot metal of the truck hood and steadied himself for the shot. The dark figure darted this way and that, then plunged into the jungle just as Bolan fired. He realized right away he had missed again.

He ejected his magazine and replaced it with a fresh one. If he had to go hunting in the African jungle, he wanted to be able to fire and keep firing without worrying how many rounds he had left.

As the Executioner went to the spot in the bushes where Lecroix had vanished, he stopped and listened. The roar of a jet engine cut through the jungle night. Then came an explosion that lifted him off his feet and threw him to the ground as if he were nothing more than a rag doll. The Executioner lay on the ground stunned. From the direction of the Katanga Swords camp came one explosion after another and then silence.

They were the last sounds the big American heard before he blacked out.

The ground shaking beneath him caused the Executioner to roll over and blink hard to get his wits back. He pushed to his hands and knees, found where he had dropped his pistol and got to his feet. The night was lit up by an incredible fire burning back at the Katanga Swords' base camp. He had no idea what had ignited to cause such an eruption, but it had to be devastating. He didn't see how many of the PMC soldiers could have escaped the violent conflagration.

He turned and looked into the jungle where Lecroix had taken refuge. If the rest of the small army had been incinerated, that left the Executioner one last chore. Jacques Lecroix had to be stopped. From all Bolan had overheard, the coup had been coming apart before he got here. N'Kruma was the hidden puppet master playing one merc against another for her own purposes. Since she already had Chimola on the hook, Bolan could only believe she wanted more than the gold deposited in the Cook Islands. Lecroix had said the account number had been given to Chimola. A mental checklist of things to do had getting that number high on the list.

After removing Lecroix.

Bolan sucked in a deep breath laden with the scent of things growing. The jungle was thick and rich with vegetation. Overlaying it came a hint of burned flesh from the Katanga Swords' camp. He plunged into the brush. The plants cut at his arms and chest as he leaned forward to bull his way through. He expected to find Lecroix's trail, but the other man had been swallowed by the dense growth. When he had gone a hundred yards, Bolan stopped to listen, since this was the only way he was likely to track Lecroix. The darkness was not quite complete, but tracking by sight was out of the question.

The jungle had fallen silent at the human intrusion. Bolan had a good sense of direction and could have retraced his steps without visual clues, but he had no intention of giving up his hunt for Lecroix. For several minutes he stood as still as a statue, and slowly the jungle noises rose around him until he was accepted as part of a vast ecosystem. He tensed when he heard a big cat roar, followed by a thrashing in the brush off to his left. A leopard hunted for a late-night dinner.

What was it after? Lecroix? If so, Bolan's work would be done for him. More likely, the big cat hunted something more familiar to its palate.

Turning slowly, Bolan found another void in the symphony of jungle noises and headed in that direction. This was the most likely spot for Lecroix to have run. Bolan worked his way through the tangle of vegetation with some effort, wishing he had a machete. But he advanced into the sound void until he heard the reason the jungle had fallen silent. Ahead, a man cursed amid the crackling of crushed brush and breaking tree limbs.

Bolan moved directly toward the sound, thinking he could get Lecroix into view and take him out.

The sudden muzzle-flash barely warned him he had fallen into a trap. Bolan sank to the spongy ground and took stock of where he might find cover. Trees provided the best chance for getting out of Lecroix's line of sight. But getting to one in spite of the lush vegetation proved harder than he expected.

Lecroix moved slowly, not sure if he had hit his target. Bolan gripped his Desert Eagle and waited for the mercenary to make a mistake. It came as suddenly as the ambush.

Lecroix rustled vines to Bolan's left, but the Executioner was not fooled. He rose and fired almost directly in front of him. The muzzle-flash revealed Lecroix holding the end of a vine he had used to decoy Bolan into reacting. The Executioner fired again but missed. Lecroix disappeared into the darkness once more.

Tracking by sounds made by his quarry no longer worked for Bolan. Lecroix knew he was being hunted and would turn the tables however he could. The Executioner sank behind a bush and duckwalked as quietly as he could, all the time waiting for any hint of where Lecroix was. The sound of feet hammering against the soft earth told him the merc had chosen to run rather than fight.

Knowing Lecroix's personality ruled out cowardice, which meant Lecroix had raced off to lay another ambush.

The Executioner was going to oblige by walking into that trap. All he needed was to recognize it first and turn it on the mercenary.

Taking a path through the thick jungle undergrowth that would bring him around Lecroix's flank took longer than he anticipated. The vines and bushes tore at him, and insects buzzed all around him. Swatting the bugs gave Bolan little relief, so he ignored them as he continued to hunt the mercenary. By the time he reached a spot where he could see more clearly through the heavy growth, he realized that Lecroix had not been intent on laying a trap. He had sought this small trail through the jungle and was now a mile or two away. To be certain, the Executioner looked closely at the bootprints and the way the trail had been marked. From all indications, this was well traveled, probably by training cadres. He started along the trail after Lecroix when he realized the sounds of the jungle had disappeared again.

Turning slowly, he saw only yellow eyes glowing in the night. Slow movement toward him brought the leopard into view. The smooth flow of muscle under the beautiful fur held no fascination for the Executioner. He lifted his Desert Eagle and waited. His eyes met those of the hunting cat. Both were killers, but Bolan was out of his normal territory and the leopard knew the jungle intimately.

The staring match went on for almost a minute before the leopard looked away, trotted a few paces, looked at him again as if sizing him up, then decided there were easier meals waiting out in the jungle. Bolan released his pent-up breath he had not realized he was holding. He lowered his pistol, glad it had not been a kill-or-be-killed confrontation. He admired the leopard, but not as an opponent that would surely die if it had come down to that.

Chafing at the wait, but knowing it was necessary, he watched the jungle for any sign the leopard was only changing its hunting tactics. When the strange noises returned, Bolan knew the hunt had moved on elsewhere.

At least the leopard's hunt had shifted. His remained the same.

Falling into a distance-devouring jog, he followed the training trail until it crossed a road marked with signs leading into Buweh. He had no idea how large the provincial capital town was, but another sign caught his eye. The governor's palace lay down a branching road. Without hesitation now, he jogged toward Joseph Chimola and, he was sure, Jacques Lecroix.

A half hour later, sweat drenching his body and causing his clothing to cling to his muscles, Bolan slowed and finally stopped to study a guard standing in the middle of the road. A tall rock wall surrounded the governor's palace, with a helipad to the side.

Bolan marched up to the guard, who swung his rifle around and called, "Stop!"

"Did Commander Lecroix enter recently? I have a message for him."

"He—" The guard never got any further. Bolan punched him hard in the belly, doubling him over. A quick knee to the chin laid out the guard on the road. Bolan dragged him out of sight and looked for other sentries. They weren't hard to find. They walked the entire perimeter of the huge estate, or were supposed to. A pair of them crouched nearby, playing cards. Another on the other side of the entrance wobbled as he walked. Too much of the local equivalent of moonshine had robbed him of his balance. Even as the Executioner watched, the guard tilted a bottle and finished it off, tossing the empty over the fence into the jungle.

Bolan walked quickly down the road, not running but knowing that a more leisurely stride would draw attention. Dawn lightened the sky and made discovery even more likely unless he looked as if he belonged. Filthy from the hike through the jungle, he might be taken for one of the Katanga Swords who had escaped their camp's destruction. At least he hoped so. He got to the front steps of the governor's palace before anyone challenged him.

A guard came around the corner as he started up the steps to the front door. Bolan turned, took in the situation and knew it was kill or be killed. The guard was not going to issue a verbal challenge—he had orders to shoot to kill.

The Executioner fired once. The mighty roar of his Desert Eagle filled the still morning air, followed quickly by the sound of a body falling to the ground. He had to move faster now, and kicked in the front doors. The tall carved wood portals swung back to let him into a marble-floored foyer. Stairs on his right spiraled to the second floor. To his left doors opened to offices. The first two rooms were empty, the third was closed. He put his hand on the doorknob and hesitated. Then he backed off. Something felt wrong.

Bolan took a deep breath, gripped his pistol and kicked in the door, immediately spinning to the side. The staccato burst from a machine gun filled the room with harsh noise, and the air with deadly lead that flew past him.

"Die, damn you!"

Jacques Lecroix fired again from inside the room. Bolan waited. The merc might go out the window, but the shrillness of his voice gave away how close to the edge of insanity Lecroix walked.

"I won't let you surrender," Bolan called.

"Who are you? You're not Chimola!"

"I'm your worst nightmare," the Executioner said.

"No, Chimola's bitch is my worst nightmare. She set me up. She destroyed my camp, killed my soldiers. She did it all to get back at me for not double-crossing him."

More bullets tore through the wall, forcing Bolan to edge along the wall. The slugs ripping past destroyed a painting, a bust on a table and tore huge gouts of plaster from the wall.

While he focused on Lecroix, Bolan was alert to other sounds. Like the ones at the head of the stairs. He moved back into the foyer and looked up, only to dive for cover when Chimola let loose with a half-dozen rounds from a pistol. He found himself trapped between Lecroix and the provincial governor.

"My guards will be here soon," Chimola called. "You are a dead man."

"You son of a bitch!" Lecroix ran headlong from the office and plunged past Bolan, never even seeing him. The mercenary swung up his machine gun and fired in Chimola's direction.

Three quick shots rang out. Bolan recognized two guns firing. He slipped into an empty room and pulled the door to, then peered out of the crack. Chimola and Coraline N'Kruma came down the stairs. Both held pistols in their hands. N'Kruma walked over to where Lecroix lay on the floor and deliberately shot him again.

"He was a fool, Joseph," she said. "It was a mistake trusting him."

"The explosions, the shooting," Chimola said, shaking his head. He appeared dazed at everything going on around him.

Bolan saw a look of hatred and contempt on N'Kruma's

face. She lifted her pistol and pointed it at the back of Chimola's head, then lowered it when the man spoke.

"I have enough offshore to last us a lifetime," Chimola said. "My helicopter. We can escape. The explosions. I don't know what happened."

"You have more money than that in the Cook Islands?"

"That's only a fraction of the gold."

Again Bolan thought she was going to shoot him.

"You know?"

"I didn't think the coup would fail, but I put some money aside. We can escape. How did the president know?"

Bolan had no idea what Chimola meant, but he saw N'Kruma come to a decision, and it was the wrong one.

"How did you know I stole from you?" she asked.

"What are you saying, my dear?"

"The account number I gave you. That was just a small deposit. I have most of it in another numbered account. I had so wanted more, but a few hundred million will have to sustain me."

She lifted her pistol and fired point-blank at the man. He staggered back and fell. N'Kruma took a deep breath, picked up the small briefcase Chimola had carried, then marched to the front door.

"Not so fast," Bolan said, coming out. He shot at her the instant he saw her catch sight of him out of the corner of her eye. She fired as fast as she could pull the trigger, but the hastily shot bullets missed. The Executioner squeezed off a round just before he found himself pinned down. Chimola's guards had finally rallied and found the courage to enter the palace.

"He killed the governor. Stop him. Kill him!"

With those words, N'Kruma ran off, leaving the guards to deal with Bolan.

It didn't work that way, though. They sprayed bullets indiscriminately. The Executioner squeezed off one well-aimed round after another and five guards died. He scrambled to the door and stepped over the bodies in time to see N'Kruma getting into a chopper at the helipad. He raised his pistol for a shot, then stopped. She half turned, lifted Chimola's briefcase to protect her body, then sank to her knees. She reached out as if trying to climb an invisible ladder, dropped the briefcase and fell facedown on the pad.

Bolan swung around and easily figured out where a sniper would have to be. The distance to the fence holding back the jungle was more than a half mile. The helicopter rose into the air without its passenger and vanished into the rising sun.

Wherever the sniper had been, he was now most likely bugging out. Bolan saw nothing to indicate the position and knew nothing of the hit other than it had been one of the best long-distance kills he had ever witnessed.

He slid back into the foyer, went to Chimola and searched the man. He carried nothing in his pockets. Whatever had been important to him had to be in the briefcase out on the helipad.

"You," came a rasping voice from behind him. "I thought I killed you in San Francisco. I won't miss again."

The Executioner dived, rolled, hit the wall and rebounded, bullets spraying around him. A chip from the marble floor seared his cheek. He came to rest on his belly, both hands supporting his Desert Eagle as he sighted on Jacques Lecroix propped against the bannister.

"That's two strikes—and you're out," Bolan said. With a bullet in his head and another in his heart, Lecroix died.

The Executioner got to his feet, took time to reload his pistol, then grabbed the machine gun Lecroix had dropped. It would come in handy getting away from this hellhole.

He fired it until it came up empty, then hurried to the helipad where N'Kruma lay unmoving. He rolled her over and saw the small spot of blood on her left breast. Shot cleanly through the heart.

Bolan scooped up the dropped briefcase and, keeping an ye out for Chimola's guards, he got over the fence and melted nto the jungle.

Kinshasa, Democratic Republic of the Congo

"We recovered much of the gold from the Cook Islands, Aaron Kurtzman reported. "The information from Chimola' briefcase helped greatly. There are other accounts we ar closing out as we speak. Well done, Striker."

Bolan lounged in the easy chair. The suite at the hotel wa lacking when compared with Claridge's or the Parker Meridiar but was a world away from the crocodile-infested Congo Rive or the heavy jungle surrounding Chimola's palace. He balance the laptop on one knee as he reached for his beer.

"What happened after I brought down the camouflag net?" he asked.

"You don't know?"

"I was occupied at the time."

"The rather clever electronic blacking they used, as well a the visual camo, disappeared. The camp showed up instantl on three different spy satellites."

"And the jet I heard was an aerial strike?"

"It took less than twenty minutes for a cruise missile to b sea launched and reach the camp. A ton of explosive warhea worked, and a second missile launch was aborted."

"I'm glad I got out when I did. Who ordered the strike?"

Kurtzman hesitated, then said, "We did not have the authority.

"CIA?"

"That is a good guess."

Bolan snorted. He was glad he had ditched the fake passport Conrad Quinn had provided and had given all the money to Antoine to help rebuild his village. That meant, however unwittingly, the CIA was helping out.

"I need a new passport to get out of the country, unless you want me to sneak out."

"We are working on it—and not using official channels."

Kurtzman had realized the problem with Quinn and the CIA. Stony Man Farm got things done and looked after their own.

"What's happened in Buweh Province?"

"Turmoil. The president of the Democratic Republic of the Congo finally realized the extent of unrest in the area and is moving to correct that. His new gubernatorial appointment is not meeting with approval from the State Department, being a longtime crony, but he is a better choice than Joseph Chimola and does not have military connections."

"No military coup, though Chimola hired the Katanga Swords."

"The members of that PMC have been dispersed. It has been decided to allow them to go their separate way and not be traced. Their organization is in shambles anyway."

"Rostov and Lecroix were the leaders. When I removed Lecroix, that ended their effectiveness as a unit."

"Agreed," Kurtzman said. There was a long pause. Then he said, "One item remains unresolved."

The Executioner sat a little straighter and looked at the rapidly changing information displayed on the laptop. After a few seconds, he broke the connection to Stony Man Farm and went to the closet. Inside was a long, narrow, heavy package holding exactly what he required to complete his mission.

THE EXECUTIONER had waited more than a day in the shabby hotel room, eye pressed to the sighting scope, waiting patiently, waiting, waiting. And Kurtzman's information finally proved true. His finger rested lightly on the .308 Galil sniper rifle he had taken from his hotel-room closet. Two figures across the busy street moved through the field of his telescopic sight.

One was tall, well dressed and carried a large briefcase. The other was skinny to the point of emaciation, matchstick arms and a face so nondescript Bolan almost forgot it the instant he saw it. But there was no need for him to remember it. He watched tiny yellow strips of cloth he had tied on a lamppost near the men to judge the wind velocity. He made a small windage change, then put his eye to the scope again.

The two men would not speak long. If the meeting went down as he suspected, they would not even acknowledge each other.

The Executioner drew back on the trigger. The rifle bucked. A second later the skinny man collapsed. He had taken out Nogomo with a single head shot.

Conrad Quinn looked around in panic, clutched the briefcase and backed away from the dead assassin. He turned and ran, looking around fearfully.

Bolan briefly considered a second shot, then drew back and began breaking down the rifle to put it into its case. His mission in Kinshasa was finished.